LENAPE HOMELAND

The Conquest series

an Indian saga volume one

James G. Landis

LENAPE HOMELAND

VOLUME ONE OF A SEVEN-PART SERIES

An Indian saga revealing the origin of a
Lenape homeland and the heroic efforts
of great sachems—Tamenend, Eesanques,
and Mattahorn—to preserve that homeland
amidst the wonders and terrors brought by
European invaders.

—as told by Owechela, a master Lenape storyteller

Illustrations by Coleen B Barnhart

ISBN: 978-1-943929-14-6 soft cover
978-1-943929-15-3 hard cover

Printed in China

TGS001247

Published by:
TGS INTERNATIONAL
P.O. Box 355; Berlin, Ohio 44610 USA
Phone: 330-893-4828
Fax: 330-893-2305
www.tgsinternational.com

Dedication

Peter Hoover

My dear friend and brother who:

» first told me the story of Isaac Glikkikan in his book, *The Secret of the Strength*.

» took me by the hand and led me to Bethlehem, Pennsylvania, for a starting look at Glikkikan's life.

» cheered me on with counsel and many an encouraging word.

» challenged me with the fullness and wonder of truth.

– James G. Landis

Overview of The Conquest Series

AMERICAN HISTORY THROUGH INDIAN EYES

James G. Landis

LENAPE HOMELAND ✦ Volume I

This story tells the early history of the Delaware Indians and the coming of the white man to the Delaware River Valley as witnessed by Lenape heroes.

HOMELAND IN MY HEART ✦ Volume II

Recounts the life story of Lenape sage, Meas, as he staggers through the events that engulf him in his homeland in the Delaware River Valley.

TOMAHAWKS TO PEACE ✦ Volume III

Glikkikan, a renowned Delaware war chief and famous orator, brings to light the hidden causes of what is commonly known as Pontiac's Rebellion.

UNDER ATTACK ✦ Volume IV

Details fierce White attacks against all Indians and the heroic attempts of Christian Indians to remain quiet and peaceable throughout.

WAR CHIEF CONQUERED ✦ Volume V

An Indian saga recounting Isaac Glikkikan's struggle to give up his former life as an influential chief, prophet, and orator and find peace in his heart.

BLACK CLOUDS OVER THE OHIOLAND ✦ Volume VI

A story of duplicity and the betrayal of the Delaware nation and the Moravian missions during the Revolutionary War.

THE FINAL CONQUEST ✦ Volume VII

Isaac Glikkikan remains stedfast in his faith amid conflict, deportation, and starvation, and at last finds a permanent homeland for his people.

Contents

» **v o l u m e   o n e** «

Lenape Homeland

Chapters

Maps & Illustrations

Maps by James G. Landis

Illustrations by Coleen Barnhart

Foreword

I first conceived of The Conquest as telling you the compelling life story of a famous Lenape war chief named Glikkikan. The scanty records tell us Glikkikan murdered an infant, led his warriors to near triumph at Fort Pitt, and as an orator for the Delaware Indians, defended the right of his people to keep their heritage and their homeland. Glikkikan converted to Christianity, became a preacher of the true Gospel, and died a martyr in the bitterness and strife of the Revolutionary War.

These bare details of Glikkikan's life lie before us as only a skeleton. They are only dead history, a collection of names, dates, and events. My task in The Conquest Series is to breathe life into Glikkikan's dried bones and give him a face you can see, a heart that throbs, and a soul that lives.

If your pulse would beat with Glikkikan's in Volume III, *Tomahawks to Peace*, you must learn to walk in his moccasins through Volume I, *Lenape Homeland*, and Volume II, *Homeland in My Heart*. You must learn of Glikkikan's past—what he believed, his culture, his heroes, his doubts, his fears.

In Volume I, *Lenape Homeland*, you will learn the origin of the fixed belief in Glikkikan's heart that the Great Spirit gave the Lenape the land along the Delaware River as their homeland. Your heart will stir with Glikkikan's when the fabled Tamenend takes the first step.

You will march with the Lenape as they advance eastward to claim the promised land and then become strong and numerous so that other tribes honor them as "Grandfather."

You will live the wonder and terror brought by the Europeans to the Land of the Lenape as Owechela tells "The Story of the Lenape" to his grandson, Glikkikan.

Your heart will thrill with Glikkikan's as you hear of the exploits of the great Sachem Mattahorn as he struggled to defend the Lenape homeland from an ever-advancing remorseless foe.

This story claims a unique role in the historical record. It presents the whole drama as seen through Lenape eyes— the eyes of smart, thinking, rational men—and not as almost always portrayed by the white historians: dumb brutes and ignorant savages.

Even most of the early artwork meant to portray to white people this ingrained bias of the observer. The artwork in The Conquest Series is intended to convey a sympathetic print of Lenape Indians as created men equal to any Europeans, not the image of some half-developed ape-man.

The Conquest Series is not a dead recording of Lenape history, but a carefully crafted story, true to the historical record, in which every character struggles with the same passions that still tug at our own hearts today.

After you weep and laugh as you follow the trails of the heroes in this story, you will never think the same way about the history of the Delaware Indians ... or about your own life. For the themes—right and wrong, good and evil—that you will ponder are timeless.

The Conquest series

volume one **Lenape Homeland**

An Indian saga
revealing the
origin of a Lenape
homeland and
the heroic efforts
of great sachems—
Tamenend,
Eesanques, and
Mattahorn—to
preserve that
homeland amidst
the wonders and
terrors brought by
European invaders.

*—as told by Owechela,
a master Lenape storyteller*

History with a heart and a face

Lenape Homeland Timeline

Historical Notes		Story Timeline	
Visigoths sack Rome	410		
		1000	Tamenend takes the first step
Beginning of Aztec & Inca Empires	1200	1200	Lenape migration to the east begins; Conquest of Alligéwi (1200–1400)
		1400	Lenape are settled in their homeland
Columbus arrives in the Caribbean	1492		
End of Aztecs—Cortez	1519		
Anabaptist movement begins	1525		
End of Incas—Pizarro	1532		
Henry VIII declares himself head of the Church of England	1534		
		1608	Champlain comes to Quebec
		1609	Hudson comes to Drunk Island
Thirty Years' War begins	1618		
		1621	Lenape become official peacemakers
		1631	Dutch settlement at Swanendael
		1638	Swedes come to the Lenape River
English Civil War	1642		
		1643	Campanius & Printz arrive
Thirty Years' War ends	1648		
English behead King Charles I	1649		
		1651	Stuyvesant takes the River for the Dutch
Istanbul, Turkey, is world's largest city	1653		
		1654	Rising retakes the River for the Swedes
		1656	Lenape commandeer Mercurius
		1657	Death of Mattahorn
Duke of York overpowers the Dutch along the Delaware River	1664		
William Penn comes to the Delaware River	1683		
William Penn returns to Pennsylvania	1700	1700	Glikkikan's birth
		1705	Owechela tells the story (1705–1708)
William Penn dies	1718		

The Story of the Lenape

Narrated by Glikkikan

I never wanted to leave my homeland along the
Lenapewihittuck.

When I say "my homeland," I mean the land all along
the Le-NAH-pay-WEE-he-tuck from its source to the Salt Sea.
The white man named this river after a governor of Virginia
who never even saw it: River De-La-Warr. I still call it the
Lenapewihittuck or the River of the Le-NAH-pay.[1]

A long, long time ago, the Great Spirit gave our people this
land. It was my homeland.

My homeland was far more than just the place where I was
born. To me it was the place where I grew up as an innocent
child reveling in the wonder of life. It was the land where I
hung my heart of love without fear of hunger, sickness, or war.

I was not afraid of hunger, for the land along the River of
the Lenape was a good land of abundant food.

From the streams we gathered sturgeon larger than a grown

---

[1] See map on page 26.

man. In the shad moon[2] we caught the shad and other smaller fish in abundance. The seas also gave up other delicacies—oysters, clams, crayfish, mussels, and scallops.

We took the deer, bear, beaver, and otter in the chase. From them we gained not only food, but also soft skins and furs to keep us warm and clothed.

The Great Spirit also sent to this good land herons, geese, ducks, and turkeys for us to eat. We enjoyed their beautiful plumage and used it to make warm blankets and delightful clothes.

In the good soil we planted the squash, the bean, the sweet potato, and the maize. And the manitos[3] sent rain to make them grow. Not only did the gardens faithfully bring forth the staples of beans, potatoes, squash, and maize, but the forest showered us with its delights—strawberries, blueberries, blackberries, plums, apples, persimmons, walnuts, butternuts, hickory nuts, chestnuts, and acorns.

I loved my homeland. It was a good land where my people were all around me. When I say "my people," I mean more than my father and mother and brothers and sisters and grandfathers and grandmothers. I mean the people of our nation who spoke the same tongue we did, dressed the same way we did, had the same black hair and the same dark eyes we did, and who worshiped the same manitos we did. Our people shared the same ancestors and the same heroes.

I call my people the LEN-nee Le-NAH-pay which means "real men." Some say it means "original people," but "real men" comes closer to its full meaning. Because the Lenni Lenape and many, many related tribes far to the north, the west, and the south of us sprang from the Lenni Lenape, the other tribes call us Grandfather. We in turn call them

[2] March is the month when the fish pass from the sea into the freshwater rivers to spawn.

[3] Spirits

Grandchildren.

The Lenni Lenape pitched their wigwams in small villages along the banks of the Lenape River and its tributaries and moved seasonally according to the hunt or the crops.

The Lenape did not build strong forts for protection as the Susquehannocks[4] to the west of us did. We were not a warlike people, but because we with our grandchildren were the most numerous and the strongest of all the nations, we did not live in fear of other nations. We treated all visitors with the greatest kindness and hospitality. We dwelled in peace in our homeland, strong and secure.

For hundreds and hundreds of years no one would ever have thought that we would have to leave the favored land the Great Spirit had given us. Then the Schwanneks[5] came—French, Dutch, Swedes, English, Irish, Germans—and they all wanted our land, until one day ... but that's my story.

I am Glikkikan. I like my name. It has a musical tapping sound to it. GLIK-ki-kan. It sounds good. But I like my name most of all because o-wee-CHEE-la gave it to me.

Owechela was the oldest man in our village. He had been around so long that he had actually talked to William Penn, the great ME-kwan,[6] as the Lenape call him. I shall never get to see the great Miquon because the last time he came to our homeland was the year I was born.[7]

[4] Lenape and Colonials alike referred to the Susquehannocks as "Minquas." This book will consistently call them "Susquehannocks" to avoid confusing them with the "Mengwe."

[5] Pronounced SHWAN-nek. A derisive term meaning "salt beings" or "bitter beings."

[6] *Miquon*, meaning "quill" or "feather" in Lenape, was a play on the English "pen."

[7] William Penn last visited Pennsylvania between December 1699 and November 1701. Glikkikan's date of birth is unknown, but my research would place it around 1700. Therefore I have chosen to use 1700 as the year of Glikkikan's birth throughout the series.—JGL

When I had seen only five winters, Owechela had seen more than eighty winters. Owechela lived by himself in a wigwam near the top of the hill above Ne-SHAM-i-nee Creek.[8] As a young boy I regularly climbed the hill to Owechela's wigwam, bringing him a piece of meat, some berries, maple sugar, or any other delicacy I could find. Many times I brought him just a gourd full of fresh water from the spring.

Owechela never tired of my coming to his wigwam and always thanked me for whatever small gift I brought him. Many other children also brought Owechela gifts and reverently offered them to him. None of us ever shouted or pushed in his presence. Owechela always thanked each one for his gift and made some comment about each child.

Owechela knew everything about each one of us. He knew the name of each one's mother, and he knew which clan— Turtle, Turkey, or Wolf—the mother belonged to. The child always belonged to the clan of the mother.

Few of the children had names at our age, but Owechela closely watched each child who came to him, and whenever he thought of a proper name that told something about the character of the child, he named that child. Owechela could think of the most beautiful names. That was one reason all the children were so respectful around Owechela. Each one hoped Owechela would give him a beautiful name.

I, too, hoped Owechela would give me a beautiful name. However, there was another reason I adored Owechela. He was the world's best storyteller. Long after the other children had gone, Owechela would tell me story after story. I would sit there in front of him looking up at his wrinkled face, his snow-white hair, and his dark eyes.

Owechela could tell stories with so much detail that I was

[8] Located in Peace Valley Park near Dublin, Pennsylvania.

sure he had been there and had seen it with his own eyes, even if it had happened long before he was born. I was sure he must have somehow seen Henry Hudson and the brave Eesanques (e SONG kees) meet the first time. I believed Owechela had somehow met Ever-Be-Joyful, Poconguigula, Eesanques, Mattahorn, and, of course, the great Tamenend. His stories made these heroes' hearts beat and my own heart pound with excitement when he told of their deeds.

Owechela could tell stories of the fox and the rabbit talking that seemed so real I did not doubt he must have heard them talking himself.

Owechela told stories about the Great Spirit and the good manitos and the evil manitos. Owechela knew all about the spirits. I wanted to please the good spirits. The evil spirits made me shiver, but Owechela told me not to worry about them because the good and bad spirits did not dwell in the same person.

The stories I liked best of all were about the Lenni Lenape and our homeland along the Lenape River.

Day after day and winter after winter Owechela told me stories. I began to notice that every time he told me a story I had heard before, the details were always exactly the same. Before many winters had passed, I could recite many of the stories Owechela told exactly as he had told them. I, too, could mimic the voice of the rabbit and the voice of the fox exactly as Owechela did.

One day when eight winters had gone by, I took my seat in front of Owechela. Owechela reached forward and placed both hands on my head. His eyes were closed and his lips moved, but all was quiet. I held perfectly still. At last, without opening his eyes, Owechela spoke:

An all-encompassing mist surrounds each one of us

when we are born. In childhood and youth we begin to lift the misty veil and peek into the past to find out where we came from and who we are.

We learn of the past through ancestors and

CQ101

traditions. We learn of people and places and forces that surround us. Because nature imposes its limits upon us, we cannot see clearly. As in a morning fog, the mist enveloping the past remains, even while the light dawns.

Owechela tells the story.

The struggle of life ensues. Storms swirl about us and shake the mighty beliefs to which we cling for protection. In turn, we fight to conquer or yield in spirit to being conquered.

We question and we search ... seeking the truth. As we stumble along through the mist, here and there we reach out and clasp in our minds a seed of truth. We clutch it to our bosom and plant it in our hearts.

We must always seek the truth. It alone can drive away the mist of ignorance that surrounds us and allow us to glimpse the path that lies ahead.

Owechela paused. His hands lay quietly on my head. I wished the music of his voice and the power flowing through the wrinkled hands would go on forever. Again Owechela spoke:

I gaze into the mist that lies ahead.

This one shall drive away the mist of ignorance for many as he searches for the truth.

His voice shall be a voice of hope for the Lenape. His words shall speak as thunder to his enemies while refreshing his people as a summer rain inspires the earth.

Good words shall jump from his lips as he speaks to and for the Lenape. Mighty deeds will mark him as a warrior and a man of renown, yet he shall fall to one greater than himself.

The hatchet, knife, and gun shall give way to the kettle, cow, and plow.

Evil shall conquer good, but the good shall triumph.

The Lenape shall lose their homeland, but he shall point them to another.

This one shall see a great distance into the past that he might gaze into the future.

This child shall use truth as the hunter uses the foremost sight on a gun barrel: to aim his weapon well. He shall aim his life by the truth. Therefore I name him Glikkikan after the foremost sight on a gun barrel.

Owechela stopped. He dropped his hands to his side and smiled.

"Glik-ki-kan. Glik-ki-kan. Glik-ki-kan." The name clicked on my tongue and danced in my head.

Owechela's smile broadened. "Do you like the name?" he asked.

"It's beautiful," I murmured. I said my name yet again. "Glik-ki-kan. I already feel five years older," I told Owechela.

Owechela began to speak very seriously to me. He had never talked to me like this before.

Glikkikan, now you are a man. Now you know that someday you will be a spokesman to and for the Lenape—an orator. You will be one whom the Lenape depend on to preserve their past. You must know every word of our past exactly as I teach it to you, and I will teach it to you exactly as I have been taught. The past must never change.

You must learn all the skills of the hunter and the warrior as well.

That is not enough. The palefaces have come to our homeland speaking in strange tongues. You must learn their tongues so that these foreigners cannot hold up the chain of friendship with one hand while stealing from us with the other.

There is much for you to learn. Your mind is supple and strong. I do not know how many winters I have left. The snow already piles on my head. I feel the days growing shorter and the nights growing longer.

Let us begin.

The First Step

As told by Owechela

The Lenape did not always dwell along the River of the Lenape. A long, long time ago the Lenni Lenape dwelled far to the west of here. Many great chiefs led the Lenape through the years from that faraway land until they settled in their homeland along the Lenape River. But the greatest chief of them all was Tamenend.

Before the time when Tamenend[9] became chief, but during the time when Salt Man and Little One were chiefs,[10] there was no rain in the land along the Yellow River[11] where the Lenape dwelled. Because there was no rain, there was no maize.

Salt Man and Little One led the people further east in search of food. When they came to the place of caves in the buffalo land, they at last had food and lived on a pleasant plain.

---

[9] Tamenend means "affable" or "affable one."

[10] Shiwapi and Penkwonwi respectively in the *Walam Olum*. The *Walam Olum* is a pictorial record of Lenape history believed by some to be true. The name means "red score."

[11] Wisawana River in the *Walam Olum*.

Salt Man and Little One ably led the Lenape through difficult times to better circumstances. The chiefs Fatigued, Stiff One, and Reprover[12] were of a different nature. Even when there was plenty of meat in the kettle, these chiefs always seemed to be out looking for dead meat with maggots in it. They were good at finding their spoiled meat and insisted on sharing it around. While Reprover was chief, the troubles got so bad that a number of angry ones stole off secretly to the east.

The wise ones who remained made Loving One[13] chief. Loving One led the people back to Yellow River, where the Lenape once again grew good maize in stoneless soil.

In this agreeable situation Tamenend became chief. His easygoing ways, his courteous manners, and his kind speech made him a friend to all the Lenape. Tamenend was the complete opposite of Reprover. Tamenend was very good for the Lenape.

Tamenend was not only gentle, kind, loving, and good; he was also very wise. He knew that one day it would turn dry again along the Yellow River and the maize would fail once more. He determined that his people should not suffer as their grandfathers had suffered in this same land. He often pondered what should be done.

This question was on Tamenend's mind each morning when he arose, stepped outside his wigwam, and faced the east. He was always there waiting—motionless, tall, erect—when the first light of dawn shoved its promise along the horizon. Then Tamenend lifted his arms upward with the index and middle fingers extended and began to chant:

---

[12] Wekwochella, Chingalsuwi, and Nekama, respectively, in the *Walam Olum*.

[13] Wakaholend in the *Walam Olum*.

Great Spirit,
Maker of the sky, the earth, the sun, the moon,
Keeper of the spirits of the fish, the birds, the animals, the
trees, the stones,
Guardian of the Four Winds,
Thank you for bringing light again to the People of the
Dawn.
Thank you for sending fire to warm our lodges and cook our
food.
Thank you for bringing water to inspire the ground and to
quench our thirst.
Thank you for the ground to grow the maize and the buffalo
to give us meat.
For the ancient song of the Lenape,
For the everlasting sun that rises this day,
I, Tamenend, the Great Sachem (SAY chem) of the Lenni
Lenape, thank you.

When Tamenend had finished his chant, he took a small pinch of tobacco from his pouch with his left hand and sprinkled it on the ground before him. Then he stood motionless with his right arm still raised and his two fingers pointed upward.

One morning while Tamenend stood there watching the dawn push the light forward, the Great Spirit spoke to him:

Tamenend. Send Strong Buffalo, Big Owl, and Willing One[14] to the dawn. I will show them a good land of never-failing waters where maize and fruits abound and where the hunter always returns with meat. I will give this land to you and the Lenni Lenape. It shall be your homeland as long as the creeks and rivers run, and while the sun, moon, and stars endure.

[14] Maskansisil, Machigokloos, and Wingenund respectively in the *Walam Olum*.

That day Tamenend stood still at that spot till the sun was high in the sky. When he returned to his lodge, he did not eat. Instead he sat quietly waiting.

The message came to Tamenend when the Lenape chiefs were gathered together for a great council fire. Hundreds of them had gathered from their villages.

Late that afternoon Tamenend made his way to the council fire and took his seat in the middle of the large half circle. When Tamenend rose to speak, every eye fastened on his eyes and every ear hung on to the great chief's words.

"Brothers," he began, "the Great Spirit has spoken and revealed his will to us. We give thanks.

"Brothers, you know that our grandfathers suffered much in this land because the rains ceased. They moved east to another home for a time, but then our fathers returned to Wisawana, where the ground is rich and without stones. But each one of us fears that the rain manito could again hold back his favor from us and we will again be in dire want. This day the Great Spirit has ordered us to go and scout another land, the Land of the Dawn.

"Brothers, the Great Spirit has chosen three men for this task, and each shall choose three more to journey with him. The way will not be easy or short, but the Great Spirit has chosen men of great gifts. He has chosen Maskansisil because he is a strong buffalo. He has chosen Machigokloos because he is wise as a big owl. He has chosen Wingenund because he is a priest and is willing.

"Brothers, when the twelve scouts return, these three chiefs will report on the land they have searched. I urge you this day to send these men out at once that they might do the bidding of the Great Spirit."

The twelve scouts left on their journey. After a long absence the twelve scouts returned and reported to Tamenend what they had seen. All twelve agreed that the land they believed to be the promised Land of the Dawn was a good land—a land abounding in game and various kinds of fruits; rivers and bays teeming with fish, tortoises, and waterfowl; and a land containing no enemy inhabitants.

But Strong Buffalo did warn of a "strong and numerous people" to the east of the Fish River.[15] He reported seeing giants that made even him look small. He told of the Alligéwi who lived in fortified cities atop huge mounds. He claimed he had seen animals much larger than a buffalo with great rolled tusks. He had even seen a very dangerous, great, hairless bear wearing such a small heart that the longest arrows could seldom pierce it.

Big Owl cautioned that it would be a very long journey to the promised land for such a huge people. He suggested just crossing the Fish River and sharing that land with the Alligéwi.

Willing One, the priest, wasn't sure that the land the scouts had visited really was the land the Great Spirit had promised them. But he was willing to go along if that was what everybody wanted to do.

Tamenend listened quietly to each report. He encouraged each scout to go on until he had given every detail of the journey he could remember. The speeches spared no words and lasted for days. Attention never lagged. As the speeches neared the end, many expected a long and detailed speech from the great chief. At last, Tamenend rose to his feet,

[15] Believed to be the Mississippi River.

turned, and faced the audience.
That fearless gentle calm his name
so aptly described seemed to
surround him.

"Brethren," he said, "the spirits
of the wind and the rain do not
deal kindly with us in this land.
Can we not leave it?

"Our scouts have told us of the
Land of the Dawn. It is a good
land. Has not the Great Spirit
given us this land?

"It is true that the journey will
be a long one. Yet even the longest
journey begins with the first step.
Can we not take it?

"There will be enemies and
dangers. But are not we the Lenni
Lenape? Are we not real men that
we should be frozen with fear?

"Watch closely and listen to my
words."

Deliberately Tamenend turned
and faced east. Then he raised his
right foot and stepped forward
while continuing to hold his left
toe touching the original spot.
Tamenend lifted both arms toward
the eastern sky with the middle
and index fingers extended. Then
he shouted:

See! I have taken the

Tamenend takes
the first step.

CQ102

first step. I have begun the journey. These bones shall never reach the Land of the Dawn, yet my spirit shall complete the journey.

True to his prophecy, Tamenend's bones rested close by the spot where he received his oracle.

Chiefs Big Owl, Strong Buffalo, and Willing One never led the Lenape away from Yellow River. But sometimes when the storm clouds towered into the sky, they could see the image of Tamenend facing the east with his arms outstretched and his right foot forward. At times when it thundered, they could even hear his shout, "See! I have taken the first step."

Chief Willing One didn't worry about the Land of the Dawn. He made huge festivals and spoke swelling words about Chief Tamenend, but he made no effort to do what the great chief had challenged the Lenape to do. That suited everyone fine.

The good times with the feasts rolled on during the times when Rich Again and Painted One[16] were chiefs. The feasting, singing, and dancing continued.

Then the good times ended and fighting broke out. The *Walam Olum* says:

- White Fowl was chief; again there was war, north and south.
- Wolf Wise-in-Counsel was chief. He knew how to make war on all; he slew Strong Stone.
- Always-Ready-One was chief; he fought against the Snakes.
- Strong-Good-One was chief; he fought against the northerners.

[16] Lapawin and Wallama respectively in the *Walam Olum*.

- Lean One was chief; he fought against the Tawa people.
- Opossum-Like[17] was chief; he fought in sadness and said, "They are many; let us go together to the Land of the Dawn. Let us carry the Spirit of Tamenend with us."

That was the beginning of the saying among the Lenape, "We carry the Spirit of Tamenend to the Land of the Dawn."

Thus began the very long journey with many encampments that brought our ancestors to the banks of Fish River. As the company trudged along day after day, at dawn each day the cry would begin in the east and roll back to the west through thousands and thousands of throats: "We carry the Spirit of Tamenend to the Land of the Dawn." The multitude would take it up again at any time during the day when a signal was needed to start or stop.

Cabin Man and Strong Friend[18] were chiefs when the Lenape started arriving at the Fish River. Both of them wanted to continue their migration to the Land of the Dawn.

Strong Friend led a delegation across the river to ask the Alligéwi if the Lenape could peacefully live in the land with them. The powerful Alligéwi would not agree to sharing the land.

Next, Chief Strong Friend asked if it might be possible to pass quietly through the Alligéwi lands and continue the journey to the east. He pointed out that the Lenape were unarmed and only an agricultural people. The Alligéwi then agreed to allow the Lenape to pass through their lands.

Having secured permission to pass through the Alligéwi lands, Chief Strong Friend and his delegation returned to the western bank of Fish River. There they began building

[17] The names of the aforementioned six chiefs and the translations given with them are found in the *Walam Olum*: Waptipatit, Wewoattan Menatting Tumaokan, Messissuwi, Chitanwulit, Alokuwi, and Opekasit.

[18] Yagawanend and Chitanitis according to the *Walam Olum*.

rafts to carry the Lenape across the river. Each day more and more Lenape arrived and pitched their camps on the western side of the river until many thousands of them waited for the crossing.

While waiting for the thousands of Lenape to arrive, the chiefs became aware of another people camped further north along Fish River. These people, called Mengwe,[19] were not so numerous as the Lenape and spoke a different tongue. The Mengwe let it be known to the Lenape that they, too, wished to migrate further east.

Meanwhile, the Alligéwi watched the thousands and thousands of migrants pouring in. They became uneasy.

When the big day arrived, Chief Strong Friend led the first fleet of rafts across Fish River. The rafts hauled well over two hundred migrants across with their few belongings and a supply of maize, and deposited them on the east bank. Then the rafts returned to the west bank to pick up the next group. Every raft performed perfectly. The travelers started a cry that jumped the river and rolled westward: "We carry the Spirit of Tamenend to the Land of the Dawn."

Chief Strong Friend led the first group a short distance inland to a campsite he had selected and began to set up camp. Then the Alligéwi appeared and mercilessly killed every one of the first Lenape band to cross over except Strong Friend. The Alligéwi stripped Strong Friend, beat him, and then let him hobble back to the riverbank.

Fired by this treachery, the Lenape built a council fire to decide what they should do. On the one hand, they were not prepared for war. They had lost a great number of men,

---

[19] Meaning "treacherous ones." Mengwe is the original name of a group of nations later called the "Five Nations" by the English and "Iroquois" by the French.

and the enemy was strong. On the other hand, they were numerous, they were not cowards, they did not want to retreat, and they wanted to possess the land the Great Spirit had given them.

The Lenape decided to invite their fellow migrants, the Mengwe, to join them in their conquest of the Alligéwi. Because the Mengwe were a much smaller group of people than the Lenape, and because they also wanted to cross the broad lands of the Alligéwi, the Mengwe readily agreed to an alliance with the Lenape. The Mengwe did insist, however, that after conquering the country, a portion of it would be theirs. Thus the two peoples struck a pact between them and vowed to conquer the Alligéwi ... or die.

And so the battle between the Alligéwi and the allied Lenape and Mengwe forces was joined. "We carry the Spirit of Tamenend to the Land of the Dawn" became the rallying cry in many a desperate battle.

No quarter was given by either side. Both sides lost many warriors. In some pitched battles when the allies stormed fortified towns, they lost hundreds of warriors; these they buried in holes or in common graves.

In these fierce battles to the death, the Mengwe always held back to the rear, leaving the Lenape to face the enemy and bear the brunt of the attack.

The Lenape scorned this cowardice on the part of the Mengwe. "Croaking frogs!" they mocked. "You Mengwe make a great noise when all is quiet, but at the first approach of danger, nay, at the very rustling of a leaf, you immediately plunge into the water and are silent."

In addition to their cowardice, the Mengwe had another troublesome practice the Lenape detested. The Lenape always spoke in whispers when they mentioned it to one another:

"The Mengwe make soup out of their enemies."

The Lenape ordered the Mengwe to stop eating the Alligéwi. "Why should we stop it?" the Mengwe protested. "The hands are bitter but the rest of it tastes like bear meat."

"We do not want to desecrate the dead," the Lenape argued. "Besides, we are the ones doing most of the fighting."

Despite the trouble in the alliance, the conquest of the Alligéwi continued year after year. Town by town and fort by fort, the Lenape and Mengwe peoples pushed ever eastward.

The *Walam Olum*, though lamentably brief, tells the tale of the struggle with the Alligéwi and the parting of the ways for the Mengwe and the Lenape:

- Sharp One was chief. They rejoiced greatly that they should fight and slay the Alligéwi towns.
- Stirrer was chief; the Alligéwi towns were too strong.
- Fire Builder was chief; the Alligéwi gave to him many towns.
- Breaker-in-Pieces was chief; all the Alligéwi go south.
- He-Has-Pleasure[20] was chief; all the people rejoice. The Lenape stay south of the Great Lakes; the Mengwe stay north of the Great Lakes.

After the separation, both nations resided peacefully for a long while; they both prospered and strengthened in numbers.

The Lenape continued their slow migration until they had spread throughout the Land of the Dawn. The Land of the Dawn stretches far along the Great Salt Sea from where the snow never falls to where the snow never melts. The people who settled this vast land are today known as Wapanachki, or

---

[20] The *Walam Olum* names these five chiefs as Kinehephend, Pimokhasuwi, Tenchekentit, Pagan Chihilla, and Hatton Wulaton.

People of the Dawn.[21]

Today, all the Wapanachki nations—Micmacs, Abnakis, Pequots, Narragansets, Mohicans, Nanticokes, Pascataway, Powhatans, and Shawnees—can understand each other's tongue, although at times it may be hard. We understand this for these nations all descended from the same Lenape people who carried the Spirit of Tamenend to the Land of the Dawn.

And right in the heart of the Land of the Dawn, the Lenape and their grandchildren—Mohicans, Nanticokes, Conoys, Shawnees, and Sapoonees—settled along the four great rivers— the Lenape River, the Mohican River, the Susquehanna River, and the Potomac River[22]—between the Alligéwi Mountains[23] and the Great Salt Sea.

In the center of all these possessions, the "Grandfather" of all the Wapanachki nations, the Lenni Lenape, settled along the streams and tributaries of the Lenape River and the Lenape Bay. There the Lenape dwelt in peace and prospered greatly in the land the Great Spirit had given them.

This land was their homeland.

Narrated by Glikkikan

Owechela was very thoughtful, kind, and patient as he taught me the story. But some spring days it was pretty hard for a boy who had seen only eight winters to spend so much

---

[21] Or "eastlanders." A loose confederation of nations stretching from the Savannah River in the south to Labrador and Newfoundland in the north. The various dialects of these Algonkian tribes were likely derived from the same primitive tongue.

[22] See map on page 26.

[23] The Allegheny Mountains.

time with Owechela. I wanted to run and play with the other boys.

Owechela would chide me, "Glikkikan, the games are soon over and the play soon forgotten. But what is carried in the head and the heart will last a lifetime."

And then we would soon be back into "The Story."

"Glikkikan, when the Lenape settled in their homeland, the Lenape children and grandchildren soon forgot the Spirit of Tamenend. The cries of 'we carry the Spirit of Tamenend to the Land of the Dawn' grew fainter and fainter. Oh yes, the people still told the story of Tamenend and of how he took the first step. The Lenape storytellers still told the story of the migration and the chiefs who had led them to this land— Opossum-Like, Strong Friend, Sharp One, Fire Builder, and Breaker-in-Pieces. But the people no longer knew the Spirit of Tamenend."

"Owechela," I asked, "what is the Spirit of Tamenend?"

"Glikkikan." The old chief bowed his head in thought.

"Glikkikan." Owechela tried once more. "Words fail me when I try to think how I can put into words what the Spirit of Tamenend is. I cannot do it now.

"But Glikkikan, I can teach you the stories of great sachems who cherished Tamenend's spirit in their own hearts ... and then ... then you will understand."

The Lenape Become Peacemakers

As told by Owechela

Whhom! *Whhom! Whhom!"*
Croaking frogs! Noisy. Harmless. If that adequately described the Mengwe, I would waste no further words. But it does not.

Mengwe, like rattlesnakes, crawl silently into your bed to share your warmth, then strike when you roll on them.

Mengwe, like buzzards, follow the wolves and feast on what others have killed.

Mengwe, like crows in pursuit of an owl, wear him thin.

Mengwe, like sly cunning weasels, steal silently upon their prey and in a flash slash the back of the neck for the kill.

Faithless, treacherous, dangerous, vicious, devious, deceitful, beastly, corrupt, cruel, crooked, disloyal, dishonest, dumb, false, gross, lying, stupid, vile, brutish, knavish, devilish, slavish—such are the Mengwe.

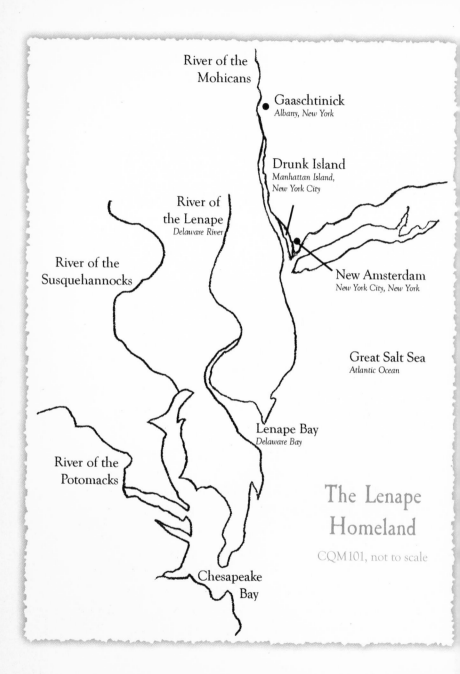

River of the
Mohicans

Gaaschtinick
Albany, New York

Drunk Island
*Manhattan Island,
New York City*

River of
the Lenape
Delaware River

River of the
Susquehannocks

New Amsterdam
New York City, New York

Great Salt Sea
Atlantic Ocean

Lenape Bay
Delaware Bay

River of the
Potomacks

The Lenape
Homeland

CQM 101, not to scale

Chesapeake
Bay

But words to describe the Mengwe fail me.

The Lenape?

They are faithful as the sun itself.

The Lenape stand strong and true as a mighty oak, changing not in the fiercest storm.

The Lenape run pure and clear as a mountain brook.

Faithful, trustworthy, honest, guileless, loyal, true, uncorrupted, gentle, noble, safe, straight, respectful, generous, stately, splendid, majestic, wise, grand, thankful, bold, courteous, manly, stalwart, free—these are the traits of the Lenape to a man.

But the Mengwe are a treacherous lot to this day.

After driving the Alligéwi out of the land, the Mengwe at first settled around the Great Lakes. In time, the Mengwe spread east of the Great Lakes, building their round-roofed communal lodges and planting large fields of maize as they moved ever closer to the Lenape and the Mohicans. The Mengwe noted the growing power of the Lenape and became concerned that the Lenape might drive them from the lands they occupied.

Their fears were not entirely unfounded. As the Mengwe looked around them—to the north, to the east, and to the south—they saw a strong and numerous people. The Lenape and their numerous grandchildren occupied lands all around them from the Fish River to the Great Salt Lake. The Lenape usually pitched only single-family round-roofed wigwams and moved easily from one site to another. They depended on fish, on the chase, and on maize for their livelihood, but they were much lighter and less dependent on one spot than the Mengwe.

In addition, the Lenape enlarged their council house and invited the Mohicans, the Nanticokes, and numerous other

of their forty grandchildren to come to their council fire.
In this way the grandchildren could benefit from the advice
of the grandfathers, and all of them could keep their family
connections alive. Live family connections also meant that
the Lenape and their grandchildren were united in a loose
military alliance to defend their homeland.

The Mengwe worried: "Will the Lenape indeed drive us off
the land we occupy?" The Mengwe began to plot how to bring
the Lenape into conflict with other distant nations. In this
warfare, not all of the Mengwe tribes acted together. Often the
individual tribes of the Mengwe peoples acted independently
of one another.

So it was that one fall day a select group of Seneca Mengwe
warriors stole off to the south toward a large fortified city
called Rique. Rique was the capital of the people of the
Panther Country.[24]

These warriors could easily have passed for just another
hunting party except for several special war clubs they carried.
These flat sticks the length of a man's arm, fingertip to elbow,
held a double-fisted ball carved on the hooked end of the
stick. On the bottom of the large ball an eyeball-sized pointed
projection stared wickedly outward. These well-balanced
weapons, when wielded by a powerful arm, could dash out the
brains of an enemy in one blow. On the handles of each of
these war clubs the Seneca warriors carried stood the fearsome
paw of a wolf and a varying number of triangular notches.
The wolf's paw marked each Seneca warrior that carried it as a
member of the Munsee tribe of the Lenape!

Although the city toward which the band headed lay along
the shores of Lake Erie only two days' journey to the south
and west of the Seneca village, the warriors had prepared for a

---

[24] The land of the Eries. The region around Erie, Pennsylvania.

long journey.

The warriors arrived at Rique shortly after dark. Two warriors quietly entered the city and murdered the first man they found outside his lodge. Then the murderer dropped the war club and ran as fast as he could go. The rest of the Seneca band fell slightly behind the lead two, protecting them in case pursuers were too numerous.

Pushing on down the Alligéwi River, the raiders continued their flight south. Once more they stopped at an Erie village, committed another murder, dropped the murder weapon, and fled.

At last the war party turned east, threaded their way across the Alligéwi Mountains, swung far to the east, and finally headed north and west. Always they traveled swiftly when moving and lay quietly when resting. Two moons later the raiders returned home.

The Eries[25] naturally concluded it had been the Munsees, the wolf tribe of the Lenape, who had attacked them, and they launched a strong and surprise counterattack. This was exactly what the Mengwe wanted.

A most bloody war resulted between the Eries and the Lenape. Erie attack and Lenape revenge. Erie revenge and then Lenape assault.

This bloody war might have gone on and on for a long time, except for Poconguigula ... and the truth.

In the days when Good-Fighter[26] was chief of the Lenape there lived among the Eries a very strong man. Although not large of stature, his strength surpassed that of any man ever known. With his knobbed war club and his amazing dexterity and strength, he could easily defeat more than a dozen of the

---

[25] The Eries occupied the region along the southern shore of Lake Erie and were wholly absorbed by other Iroquoian-speaking tribes such as the Hurons, the Wyandots, and the Senecas.

[26] Wulitpallat according to the *Walam Olum*.

strongest men of the time. Because of their confidence in the strong man's strength, the Eries challenged the Lenape to a duel between only twelve chosen warriors from each side. The strong man, of course, would command the Erie warriors.

The Erie challenge very much disturbed the Lenape war chiefs and braves gathered together in council. The chiefs and braves wanted to accept the challenge, but all feared it would be a terrible disaster.

While the council pondered what to do, a young man, Poconguigula, came in to the council and offered, "I will go and bring the Erie strong man to this place as a prisoner. I ask only for five brave warriors to go with me."

Because Poconguigula had never distinguished himself as a brave, or in any other way, the chiefs and warriors laughed at him and Chief Good Fighter told him, "We need no baby in this game. The Erie strong man is equal to twenty ordinary men. Even if you find him asleep, how can you, a mere boy, with just five men, hope to do anything with the Erie strong man?"

"Great Chief," said Poconguigula, "it is true that I am young and have never fought in battle, but I have spent much time alone with the manitos. One day as I sat alone in the forest, I saw a rattlesnake lying on the open ground beneath a tree. From the lower limb of a great tree, a catbird taunted the snake. The snake did not move. It only fastened its eyes on the bird and stared at it. The bird's calls grew weaker until they became still. At last the catbird fell from the limb and lay helpless in front of the rattlesnake.

"Great Chief, I will use the power of the snake's eyes to make the Erie strong man powerless."

"Little One, have you indeed discovered the power of the snake's eyes?" asked Chief Good Fighter.

"Great Chief, I have indeed faced a she-bear with two half-grown cubs. She wanted the fish I had taken from the river. But the power of the snake's eyes was too strong for her. The she-bear lay down along the path and allowed me to continue walking quietly past her. The two cubs ran off into the woods.

"Great Chief, the strong man will be no different than the she-bear. I have had assurance from Waymahtahkuneese[27] that I will prevail over the strong man. Just give me the five men, and I will show you what I can do."

Chief Good Fighter and the council, doubting they would ever see Poconguigula or any of the five brave warriors again, decided to let Poconguigula go.

As soon as it was decided that he could go, Poconguigula and his little party gathered their supplies along with plenty of strong cord and set out. After days of travel, they arrived at the Erie village. The warriors entered the village at night, killed a man, and left a plain trail so they could easily be followed.

The next morning the Eries discovered the murder and found out that only six braves were in the party. They sent the strong man with a dozen braves to follow and capture the offenders. This was exactly what Poconguigula wanted. He left his escort a little behind him concealed in some undergrowth, and approached the Eries alone. In an open clearing, he stood and faced the war party. The strong man advanced toward Poconguigula alone while the rest of his party watched from the edge of the clearing.

When the strong man was quite a distance away from him, Poconguigula locked his eyes on the strong man's eyes. The strong man slowly wilted. Poconguigula called his men to him and told them, "Bind the strong man with the cord, place him on a litter, and bear him to the Lenape."

[27] "The Little Warrior." This legendary character always protected the Lenape in time of war.

Poconguigula and the power
of the snake eyes

The other terrified Erie warriors just stood there helplessly looking on. They soon returned to the tribe and told the Eries what had become of their leader.

Poconguigula kept the strong man under his influence until early the next morning. Then he said to the five warriors, "I must now get some rest. Guard the strong man carefully while I retire."

While Poconguigula rested, the strong man recovered his senses, broke the thick cords, and started home. When the five braves saw him regain his strength, they ran for their lives.

Poconguigula immediately followed the runaway, and by his strange power soon brought the strong man back and had him bound again.

Without further mishaps the war party arrived at the Lenape village. Poconguigula delivered his prisoner to Chief Good Fighter.

"Great Chief," he said, "I have done my duty. With the help of Waymahtahkuneese I have delivered the prisoner."

Without further words or description of his brave journey, Poconguigula retired to his wigwam.

A short time after Poconguigula withdrew his influence, the Erie strong man recovered, broke his prisoner cords again, and, defying everybody present, walked away. Chief Good Fighter quickly called Poconguigula and sent him after the strong man again. Poconguigula followed him and soon subdued him once more. He took the Erie to his own tent and had the strong man wait upon him with apparent pleasure.

The next day Poconguigula told the strong man, "You may now return to your own country. Please advise your people to send their chiefs and warriors to the Lenape at once and make a treaty of friendship. With a strong man such as the

Eries have in you, and with a power such as I possess for the Lenape, we would be able to overcome any enemy that might choose to make war against either of us."[28]

The Erie chiefs and warriors did return to the Lenape, bringing with them a special wampum belt. It was not the usual peace belt made only of strings of white conch shells. The strings of this belt passed through a beautiful copper heart in the center of the belt, with the white shell-beads glistening on both ends.

The Erie orator read the message of the belt:

"The Lenape and the Erie people shall now be a people of one heart. It is a heart of peace. Today, you shall examine the belt and see if the heart is true and unchangeable."

Here the orator stopped and gave the belt to the chief closest to him. The chief examined the belt closely. "The heart is true and unchangeable," the chief declared. Then he passed the belt on to the next chief. That chief examined it, made the same declaration, "The heart is true and unchangeable," and passed the belt on to the next chief.

After every chief had found the heart to be true and unchangeable, the orator again took the belt and continued:

"As long as this heart does not change, we shall be two nations with one heart of love. The Lenape shall watch this belt and examine it at your council fires to see whether the heart changes. As long as the heart does not change, all shall know that the Eries remain the friends of the Lenape."

In this way both Eries and Lenape pledged for themselves and for their posterity a defensive and offensive alliance.

Now that the Eries and the Lenape had made a peace treaty, they discovered that the real cause of the war had not been the Lenape at all. It had been the Mengwe, who again had lived

[28] This story is adapted from Legends of the Delaware Indians, by Richard C. Adams.

up to the meaning of their name: "the treacherous ones."

Both nations now sought to avenge themselves of the Mengwe treachery. Chief Good Fighter proved to be an able leader and warrior for the Lenape. He led many large parties to the north and savagely attacked the Mengwe. The Lenape fought with great vigor and determination, for it lay strong in their hearts to wipe out this deceitful race. The Mengwe trembled.

Up to this time, the tribes of the Mengwe—Senecas, Onondagas, Oneidas, Mohawks, Cayugas—fought independently of one another. But now, to escape extermination one tribe at a time, the chiefs held a great council fire and organized a confederacy among them later known by Europeans as the Five Nations. In reality, it was only the five tribes of one nation, the Mengwe. The Lenape still call them Mengwe or Mingos.

By forming the confederacy, the Five Nations thus united their forces against the Lenape. When the Mengwe made their alliance,[29] the Lenape still could have destroyed them if they had persisted in their warring, for the Lenape then were as numerous as grasshoppers and as destructive to their enemies as these insects are to the fruits of the earth when they swarm upon them.

But there were other forces at work that kept the Lenape from continuing the wars with the Mengwe for a time. Another Tamanend came on the scene who understood the advantages of peace. The *Walam Olum* tells us: "Again an Affable was chief, and made peace with all. All were friends, all were united, under this great chief."[30]

"There is never victory in war," Tamanend said. "There is

[29] The Five Nations Confederacy took place in 1570.

[30] *Lappi tamenend sachemanepit wemi langundit. Wemi nitis wemi takwicken sachema kichwon.*

only the destruction of both peoples. The victor drains the blood from the veins of the vanquished, but alas, in doing so, he severs the sinews that bind his own heart in place.

"Come, remember," Tamanend would say. Then he would shout, "We carry the Spirit of Tamenend in the Land of the Dawn."

In this way Tamanend sought to rally the people and urge them to lay aside their quarrels with other nations. A general peace for the Lenape lasted during his lifetime.

But blood feuds continue easily from one generation to another. Hatred passes naturally from father to son, and the desire to avenge past wrongs inflames the hearts of young braves.

And so the wars between the Cherokees and the Lenape resumed. Just as in the wars between the Eries and the Lenape, the Mengwe first poisoned the root of the Cherokee tree with stray raids and deceptive war clubs. Then when the Lenape went out to avenge the Cherokee assault, the Mengwe secretly joined in the attack against the Lenape. Thus the ongoing feud with the Cherokees also prevented the full might of the Lenape from crushing the perfidious Mengwe.

Back and forth the battles raged for many years as the blood feud continued between the Lenape and the Cherokees. Both sides tired of the raids, the killings, and the plunder, but honor demanded that neither braves nor chiefs from either side could offer the peace belt to the other.

Into this political impasse one of the tender and compassionate sex stepped forward to be the peacemaker.

A large hollow log with a deerskin stretched tightly across

both ends rested on stones outside the council lodge. The drummer pounded his wooden mallet against the taut deerskin: *Bom-m-m-m*. The deep bass note rolled from the hilltop and spread through the surrounding woods.

Down by the river to the east a single female voice answered, "Oh, Wa-a-a-a." The "Oh" rang out two octaves higher than the drum. The plaintive cry, "Wa-a-a-a," sounded on the note "la."

The drummer swung his hammer again. *Bom-m-m-m*.

This time one hundred female voices answered the drum: "Oh, Wa-a-a-a."

Bom-m-m-m. This time the lone voice again, "Oh, Wa-a-a-a." *Bom-m-m-m*. This time the hundred voices, "Oh, Wa-a-a-a."

The cadence continued. Always the drum sounded first, followed by the single voice; then the drum again, followed by the hundred voices.

Bom-m-m-m. "Oh, Wa-a-a-a." *Bom-m-m-m*. "Oh, Wa-a-a-a." *Bom-m-m-m*. "Oh, Wa-a-a-a." *Bom-m-m-m*. "Oh, Wa-a-a-a"...

Very slowly the wailing chorus moved ever closer to the council lodge. Each drumbeat brought the procession one step closer.

In the lead moved the lone voice, a forty-year-old woman with head and eyes upturned. The well-moistened hollow face, deep-set eyes, and listless bearing marked her as one in deep grief. Yet even in her deep grief she carried herself with a dignity that set her apart as a mother of chieftains. Her skirt and long-sleeved shirt both were made from the finer feathers taken from the turkey breast and intricately interwoven with hemp thread, such that as the woman moved, the sheen on her garments appeared first brown, then bronze, then gold, then black, then jade. A single narrow band of brilliant red followed the border of her collar, cuffs, shirt bottom, and the edge of her blanket-skirt. She wore deerskin leggings and moccasins trimmed with that same brilliant red border. A gold pendant hung from the chain around her neck. A small silver earring dangled from each ear. A wide deerskin belt with repeating designs and a large silver buckle clasped her shirt tightly around her girth. Her black hair flowed gently over her shoulders and covered the belt in the back. Draped over her outstretched right hand lay a wampum belt of 1,379 white shell-beads. In her open palm she held the copper heart embedded in the belt.

Bom-m-m-m. "Oh, Wa-a-a-a." Bom-m-m-m. "Oh, Wa-a-a-a." Bom-m-m-m. "Oh, Wa-a-a-a." Bom-m-m-m. "Oh, Wa-a-a-a"...

The dirge continued as the hundred-voice escort followed the lead woman at a close but respectful distance, pitching their plaintive cries upward in response to her wail, while ever stepping forward at the beat of the drum.

The lone woman stopped moving when she reached the entrance of the lodge, but continued her mournful solo while her escort, step by step and drumbeat by drumbeat, formed a complete circle around the lodge.

When the circle around the lodge was complete, the drummer stopped and the wailing ceased.

A lone chief pushed aside the lodge skin, took the woman lightly by the arm, and guided her into the dimness of the council lodge. He gently pushed her toward the center of the semicircle where the chiefs were seated, Cherokee chiefs on one side and Lenape chiefs on the other. Then he resumed his seat and bade her speak.

"I am Ever-Be-Joyful, and I am come before this joint council fire of the Lenape and Cherokee nations. I do not want to be here. I would rather hold my peace as I have for the past twenty and five winters. But to have my son scorched and roasted by fire, his scalp torn from his head, and his ashes trampled in disdain has unloosed my tongue. I can no longer be silent.

"When my son left on the warpath, he prayed to the Great
Spirit:

O Great Spirit! Take pity on poor me
Who am going out to fight the enemy.
I know not if I may come again with life
And enjoy the embraces of my children and my wife.
    And I will make thee a sacrifice.

O Great Spirit! I am but a creature poor
Who has no power to secure
My life and limb with my own hands,
But have given them to duty and to the nation's bands.
    And I will make thee a sacrifice.

O Great Spirit! Take pity on my children and my wife.
Keep them from mourning for my life.
Grant that I may successful be
In this attempt to slay my enemy.
    And I will make thee a sacrifice.

O Great Spirit! Help me bring home the trophies of war,
That I may come carrying scalps and flesh and more
To my dear friends and family.
That we may in honor be glad at our great victory.
    And I will make thee a sacrifice.

O Great Spirit! Take pity on me!
Give me strength and courage to meet my enemy.
Suffer me to return again to my children and my wife.
Take pity on me and preserve my life.
    And I will make thee a sacrifice.

"Yes, my son has made a sacrifice." Ever-Be-Joyful waited while fresh tears rolled down over her cheeks. Then in a thick voice she went on. "He has sacrificed his own blood. His scalp has become the trophy of war that he asked the Great Spirit to give him."

Again she struggled to gain control of herself before going on. "And for what noble purpose did my son give his hair? Are his wife and children better fed? Is the Cherokee brave who slew my son happier because he carries the bloody trophy in his belt? Will that brave's children eat more venison and be better clothed because he has slain my son?

"Will the blood of my son bring peace that the wailing of the widow and the mother may cease? Nay. Cold blood brings forth hot blood, and honor demands that the blood of my son be avenged.

"Today, I, a mere woman, am not bound by honor. I, Ever-Be-Joyful, am bound by grief. Call me Ever-Be-Joyful no longer. Now you shall call me Ever-Be-Sad, for I now know that all my labors rearing this son have been wasted, slain in quest of so-called bravery and honor. This my son was alive. Now he is dead.

"Honor says that men must be brave and strong; men must remain unswayed by pain or fear, tenderness or tear. Men never know the gripping pains that engulf a woman who goes out into the woods to give birth to a baby. It was I who suffered that pain and brought forth my son. The agony of the pain lasted all through the day and on into the night. Fainting and exhausted, I felt I must perish before my first son was born. But he came, and I joyfully held him in my arms and nursed my son.

"I gladly gave of my own body and strength to care for my son. It was I who planted the maize. It was I who suffered blistered hands to care for it, and it was I who gathered it and cooked it that my son might have *sappan*.[31] It was I who toiled through the snow to drain the sap from the maple tree and boiled it that my son might taste sweetness. It was I who dressed the deer and stirred the fire that my son might savor venison. It was I who wore my fingers raw scraping the hides that my son might wear the best of moccasins and the softest of shirts. It was I who stood by at night and bathed his fevered body when sickness attacked my son. I gladly suffered each hardship for the sake of my son. I would gladly have given my very life to protect him.

"Alas, it was all for honor ... for nothing. I would rather my son had life than this useless honor. Call me Ever-Be-Sad."

Once more Ever-Be-Joyful let the tears flow and waited to regain her voice. Then she went on: "I do not suffer alone. There are few among these brave warriors gathered around this council fire who have not known the loss of a son, a brother, a friend. That is bad enough. But can you not take pity on your wives and children and stop this senseless feud? Grieve for wives who have no one to hunt for them. Grieve for children who have no one to protect them. Grieve for mothers who have poured their very strength and life into a son only to see him flung into the grave.

"All have known the agony of a loved one torn from their arms for the sake of honor. And I ask you, of what worth are the trophies of those slain in battle? Would it not be of far greater worth to have arms about you to protect you, to care for you, and to hold you close?

"So I pray that warriors might have their fill of bravery and honor. And I ask, is it really bravery to tie a helpless victim to a stake, light a fire under him, and then taunt him while he

---

[31] A cooked mush made of pounded Indian corn.

"I am not bound by honor,
I am bound by grief." —Ever-Be-Joyful

roasts? Is enduring the smell of burning flesh what you call bravery?

"You have been brave enough. You have enough of honor. Let the Cherokees and the Lenape bury the hatchet and stop destroying one another while the Mengwe, the treacherous ones, mock us saying, 'Ah, the Cherokee and the Lenape warriors are so-o-o brave.'

"I adjure every warrior by everything that is dear to him: take pity on the sufferings of your wives and helpless infants; turn your faces once more toward your homes, families, and friends; forgive the wrongs suffered from each other; lay aside your deadly weapons, and smoke together the pipe of amity and peace.

"Both sides have shown sufficient proofs of courage; both contending nations are alike high-minded and brave. Now you must embrace as friends those whom you have learned to respect as enemies.

"I hold before you the belt of friendship the Eries gave us long ago. Please examine it this day and see if the heart has changed. Can this heart not be large enough to include the Cherokee nation?

"I beg you. Make the death of my son a memorial to the friendship of these two nations. Restore to me my name, Ever-Be-Joyful, that there might again be a spring in my step, a light on my face, and a song in my heart."

So saying, Ever-Be-Joyful knelt before the chief who had ushered her in, laid the wampum belt in his lap, and slipped quietly from the lodge.

As soon as she exited the lodge, the drummer once more swung his mallet against the taut deerskin. *Bom-m-m-m.* Ever-Be-Joyful let out that doleful cry: "Oh, Wa-a-a-a." *Bom-m-m-m.* The hundred voices answered, "Oh, Wa-a-a-a," and the return march to the east began.

No warrior could resist the impassioned pleading of Ever-Be-Joyful. The Cherokees and Lenape smoked the pipe of amity and peace as she had pled with them to do. Now the Lenape could continue their onslaught against the Mengwe with renewed vigor. In these bitter battles the Lenape generally came off victorious, but every victory came with a price paid in dead and wounded. The Lenape still were not strong enough to crush the Mengwe.

Help for the Lenape war to eradicate the treacherous Mengwe appeared far to the north of the Lenape homeland. The French[32] began to arrive and build trading posts and settlements on the northern edge of the Mengwe settlements. On a river the Mengwe call The Big Waterway,[33] a Frenchman named Champ Gun[34] built a fort and a storehouse. The first winter proved extremely cold, and only eight of Champ Gun's twenty-four settlers survived.

In such a weakened state, Champ Gun wanted to show himself friendly to the surrounding Huron and Algonquian peoples so he could trade furs with them and explore their country further. In an effort to win the lasting friendship of the surrounding peoples, Champ Gun and two of his friends went along with the natives in a raid against the hated Mengwe to the south of them.

Champ Gun and his two friends carried muskets. The

---

[32] In 1608 a Frenchman named Samuel de Champlain sailed up the Saint Lawrence River to Quebec, a place the local Algonquian people called kebec, meaning "the place where the river narrows."

[33] Kaniatarowanenneh in the Iroquois tongue. The Saint Lawrence River.

[34] Samuel de Champlain.

Mengwe knew nothing of muskets, and the attackers easily defeated them. Champ Gun accomplished his goal: by this raid he made lasting friends of the Hurons and Algonquians ... and something he did not intend; he made lasting enemies of the Mengwe.

The Lenape were delighted at this turn of events. Now the French would tip the balance of power in their favor in their fight with the Mengwe.

The Mengwe, too, understood their own dilemma. They had powerful enemies on both sides. The Algonquians and Hurons to the north allied with the French, and off to the south and east were the Lenape and their forty grandchildren.

The Lenape and the French began embracing the Mengwe in one great big bear hug, and the Mengwe began gasping for air. If the Mengwe did nothing about it, they would soon be forced to leave their well-established villages to the south of The Big Waterway and journey far inland.

Moving was not an option for the Mengwe, so the Mengwe chose another way to continue their treachery.

Let me tell you about the coming of the Dutch to Manahachtánienk.[35] To this day, the Lenape still call the place Drunk Island. Up to this time, the Lenape and their relatives, the Mohicans living in the area, knew nothing of white men and nothing of rum.

In that fateful year[36] an Englishman named Henry Hudson sailed along the coast, exploring. Because Dutch merchants financed his voyage, Holland claimed the lands Hudson

[35] Manahachtánienk means "The place where we all became intoxicated." Manhattan Island, New York.

[36] Henry Hudson's third voyage in 1609.

"discovered" as their own, and the settlers, traders, and soldiers who followed Hudson to our homelands were Dutch.

The story of how the Lenape welcomed the Dutch to Drunk Island is very firmly fixed in our tradition, and the details are well remembered in our legends.[37]

Some Lenape were out fishing where the sea widens when they spied Hudson's ship far out at sea. They had never seen anything like it before and immediately returned to shore. They urged others to go along out to sea with them and see if they could discover what it might be.

They hurried back out on the great water and studied with wonder what now appeared to their sight, but they could not agree what it was. Some thought it to be a large fish or animal, whereas others thought it must be a large house floating on the water.

At length they concluded that the object was moving toward the land and must be some kind of animal or something else that had life in it. Accordingly, they felt it proper to notify the chiefs of the surrounding islands what they had seen, urging them to send warriors hither immediately.

The warriors and chiefs arriving in great numbers saw for themselves the strange object as it moved slowly toward the entrance of the river. They concluded it must be the house of the Manito,[38] Keeshaylummookawng, and that Keeshaylummookawng himself was coming to visit them.

Now a great amount of confusion ensued. All wondered, "What is the proper way to receive Keeshaylummookawng?" The natives gathered plenty of meat for a possible sacrifice to appease the Manito if he was angry. The women prepared the best victuals. The magicians examined all the idols and

---

[37] History, Manners, and Customs of the Indian Nations, John Heckewelder, pp. 71-75.

[38] Supreme Being.

images and put them in order. The young people proposed a grand dance as a suitable entertainment for the Great Being. The conjurers set to work to determine the meaning of this visit and what the results of it might be. Men, women, and children, torn between fear and hope, looked to the chiefs and wise men for advice and protection.

In the midst of all this uncertainty and activity, the large canoe finally arrived. A smaller canoe carrying several men pushed off from the larger canoe; one man was dressed in a red coat glittering with gold lace. Surely, the Lenape thought, this must be the Manito himself. "But," they wondered, "why should he have such a white skin?"

The chiefs and wise men gathered themselves into a large circle toward which the supposed Manito and two others approached. With friendly signs and motions, the red-clothed Manito greeted the Lenape chiefs. With the chiefs standing around him in a circle, the Manito's helper poured a glass of an unknown drink, and the Manito drank it. Then the helper refilled the glass, and the Manito handed it to the chief standing next to him. The chief took one smell of the drink and handed it to the chief standing next to him. This chief passed it to the one next to him, and thus it went all the way around the circle.

Just before the glass was about to be returned to the red-clothed Manito, a brave chief named Eesanques jumped up and spoke to the assembled natives. "The cup was handed to us by the Manito, and he intends us to drink from it as he himself has done. If we do not follow his example, the Manito may be provoked to wrath and bring destruction upon us. I am not afraid. For the good of the nation I will drink from the cup, come what may. It is indeed better for one man to die than for the whole nation to be destroyed."

Eesanques stopped, reached out his hand, and waited for the glass to be handed to him. Everyone present—men, women, and children—fixed their eyes on Eesanques as the cup came to him. Eesanques held the cup high that all might see, and in a strong voice he proclaimed, "I bid you farewell." Then Eesanques lowered the cup to his lips and drained the whole cup.

Soon Eesanques began to stagger, and everyone watched in horror as he fell prostrate on the ground. Thinking he had died, his companions began to bemoan the brave chief's fate.

Then Eesanques woke from his sleep and declared, "I have never felt so happy in my whole life as when I drank the cup. I cannot describe the sensations I have enjoyed. I wish to have some more of the drink."

The supposed Manito granted Eesanques his wish, and then the whole assembly followed the chief's example and drank from the cup until they all became intoxicated.

During the general intoxication, the white men confined themselves to their vessel. Then the man with the red clothes returned to the shore. The Manito made it clear to everyone that he was very pleased with them. He gave the Lenape presents consisting of beads, ax heads, hoe heads, and stockings such as the white men wear. By using signs, the Manito made the red men understand that he was going away, but that in about one year he would return again.

The Lenape had no idea how to use the gifts the Manito had given them. They put them away most of the time. At their special feasts they would get the ax heads and hoe heads out and hang them as ornaments around their necks. The stockings they used as tobacco pouches.

In about a year the Dutchmen returned to Drunk Island. The Lenape saw them coming and proudly wore their ornaments about their necks. The Dutchmen laughed at the Lenape. Then they showed them how to make handles for the axes and cut down trees in front of their eyes. The Lenape marveled at such a wonder, and this further convinced them that they had been honored by a visit from their gods.

After several encounters, the Lenape began to realize that their visitors were not gods, but men like themselves from a faraway country. Familiarity increased daily between the Dutch and the Lenape until one day the Dutch asked for "a small piece of land in order to sow some seeds and raise herbs to season their broth." The Dutch asked for only as much land as the skin of a bull would cover and then spread a bull hide on the ground in front of the Lenape to show its size. Thinking the request reasonable, the Lenape agreed to it.

Immediately, a Dutchman took a knife and, beginning at one place on the hide, cut it into a rope no thicker than the finger of a little child. When he was done there was a large coil. This hide rope was then drawn out to a great distance and brought around so that both ends would meet, and it encompassed a large piece of land. The Lenape were surprised by the superior wit of the Dutch, but they did not complain about allowing their guests to have this small plot of land, because they still had more than they needed.

But the Lenape should have known better. After all, the Dutchman had said he wanted only a "little, little land, on which to raise greens for his soup, just as much as a bullock's hide would cover." Here they first might have observed the Dutchman's deceitful spirit. When the bullock hide was cut up into little strips, and did not cover, indeed, but encircled a very large piece of land, the Lenape should have known. The Dutch were to raise "greens" on it; instead, they planted "great guns" on it. After that they built strong houses and made themselves masters of the island.

The Dutch traded with the Lenape. They brought valuable cloth, pots and kettles, tools ... and guns. The Lenape marveled at the wonderful inventions of the white man. An iron or copper cooking kettle outlasted ten clay pots. Duffel cloth was so much lighter than blankets and robes of animal skins. Knives and axes made of iron held their edges much better than rocks or bones. The Lenape saw the great advantages of the Dutch trade goods and wanted them. The Dutch wanted peltries and maize from the Lenape. The Lenape freely traded with the Dutch.

Guns were another matter. The Dutch did not want the Lenape to have guns. At first the Lenape did not really want guns because they knew that guns scared the game and often needed repairs. Many hunters still preferred to use the bow and arrows. Both the Dutch and the Lenape knew that in warfare guns could provide a decisive advantage. But the Lenape did not want to fight; they wanted to trade.

The trade between the Dutch and the Lenape increased rapidly. The Dutch West India Company sent hundreds of boatloads of skins and furs back to Europe. So did the French. And the English wanted their fair share of the market.

Each fall and winter when the skins were in their prime, skilled Lenape hunters spread out through the woods to supply the seemingly limitless demand for peltries. Instead of killing beavers and deer just to supply their own needs as they had done before, the hunters killed everything with a marketable pelt. A good hunter might kill five, six, or seven deer each day plus many raccoons, beavers, otters, wildcats, and other animals.

The depletion of game that followed such slaughter meant that in just a few years it became much harder to find the game. Hunters had to go farther from home to find the game, and this meant they often encroached on hunting lands of other tribes.

For the Lenape, the shortage of game along the Lenape River meant they had to go west into the Susquehanna Valley to find better hunting. The Susquehannocks resented such encroachment and launched raids against the Lenape. At times the Mengwe, applying their old trick of leaving false evidence against the Susquehannocks, also attacked a Lenape hunting party, killed the hunters, and made off with the peltries. This happened more than once or twice. In fact, it was so bad that if any Mengwe were found on Lenape lands, he was killed as soon as caught.

For the Mengwe, obtaining furs had become a matter of survival. They, like the Lenape, quickly depleted the hunting grounds around their native lands and now depended on trade for their new way of life instead of living off the land as they formerly had done. The French and the Hurons controlled the fur trade to the north and far to the west of the Mengwe. The Lenape, Mohicans, and Susquehannocks continued their onslaught against the Mengwe from the east and the south.

Thus the killings and wars continued, red men against red men, while the French, Dutch, and English invaded the country and claimed it for their own.

In this desperate situation, the Mengwe sent messengers carrying wampum belts to the Lenape villages along the Lenape River. These were the messages the Mengwe messengers gave to the chiefs at each place:

Message One:
We know there have been long and bitter wars
between the many Indian nations. We know it is not

profitable that all the Indian nations should be at war with each other; this will at length be the ruin of the whole race of red men. The facts seem simple and plain. Continued wars among us will weaken and destroy the Indian nations.

Message Two:

The field of battle is always overshadowed by the vice of hate. Hate does not see clearly. Hate blinds us to greater danger. We must not be like two bucks so enraged in the fight with each other that they both fail to see the cliff's edge; then both bucks fall from the cliff to their death below. Let us wipe hate from our eyes that we may see the cliff's edge. Why should the nations of the red man continue to destroy each other when much more powerful and dangerous nations have come to our shores?

Message Three:

We know that among us honor demands that we do not hold forth the peace belt with one hand while firmly clutching the bloody hatchet in the other. For a peace of bitterness lasts only until the contestants have renewed their strength. A man's thoughts and actions should be of one piece. Good and evil never dwell together in the same man. For all of these compelling reasons, our tradition dictates that a warrior cannot and shall not offer peace to enraged combatants, no matter how compelling the reason. So the question is, "How can we listen to the voice of reason and still have peace with honor?"

Message Four:

We have therefore considered a remedy by which the evil of continued warfare may be prevented. One

nation shall be "the woman." We will place her in
the midst, and the other nations who make war shall
be the man, and live around the woman. No one
shall touch or hurt the woman, and if anyone does,
we will immediately say to him, "Why do you beat
the woman?" Then all the men shall fall upon him
who has beaten her. The woman shall not go to war,
but endeavor to keep peace with all. Therefore, if the
men who surround her beat each other and the war
be carried on with violence, the woman shall have
the right of addressing them like this: "Ye men, what
are ye about? Why do you beat each other? Consider
that your wives and children must perish, unless you
desist. Do you mean to destroy yourselves from the
face of the earth?" The men shall then hear and obey
the woman.

Message Five:

The role of the woman in being a peacemaker is
one of honor. When the tender and compassionate
sex comes forward, yea, when the woman comes
forward and holds out the peace belt, warriors may
honorably bury the hatchet deep underground. This
feat of the woman shows not her weakness, but her
strength; it shows not her cowardice, but her courage;
it shows not her frailty, but her vigor; and it shows
not her infirmity, but her nobility.

To be a peacemaker is a place of honor that no
warrior can fill. It is a place that no weakling can fill,
for the contestants will pay the woman no mind.

Message Six:

The Mengwe have deeply reflected on the critical
situation of the Indian race. We know that the

role of the woman cannot be taken by a weak or contemptible tribe, or the other tribes would not listen to her. This role must be given to a nation that at once commands respect and possesses influence.

The Lenni Lenape and their allies are such a nation. As men, they have been dreaded; as women, they would be respected and honored. None would be so daring or so base as to attack or insult them. As women, they would have a right to interfere in all the quarrels of other nations and to stop or prevent the spilling of Indian blood.

Message Seven:

We, the Mengwe, entreat you, the Lenni Lenape, to become "the woman" in name and to throw down the weapons of war and all the insignia of warriors, to devote yourselves to agriculture and other pacific employments, and to thus become the means of preserving peace and harmony among the Indian nations.

Thus, as "women," the Lenni Lenape may enjoy the respect and submission of all the Indian nations while reaping the fruits of peace in the Land of the Dawn that the Great Spirit has given you.[39]

The Lenape yielded to the appeal and the flattering words of their mortal enemies, the Mengwe. They agreed to accept the honor of being "the woman" and become the peacemaker among the Indian nations.

After the Lenape agreed to accept the honor, the Mengwe invited the Lenape and the Mohicans to a grand council some

---

[39] *History, Manners, and Customs of the Indian Nations*, John Heckewelder, pp. 57-59.

distance from Gaaschtinick[40] on the Mohican River.[41]

At the grand council[42] the Mengwe appointed a great feast accompanied by many speeches and fitting ceremonies. The Mengwe orators presented no less than twenty wampum belts to the Lenape, each belt bearing its own embedded meaning.

When the Lenape and the Mohicans from Drunk Island arrived at the grand council near Gaaschtinick, they were surprised to find the Dutch were there also. But they soon understood. Dutch guns would enforce the new treaty.

Many chiefs of the nation attended the council fire, including Eesanques. It was Eesanques who preserved for the Lenape the words of the Mengwe oratory. I shall recite here only parts of the most important speeches given by the Mengwe orators.

Cousins and Nephews:

You came a great way to visit us, and many sorts of evils might have befallen you by the way which might have been hurtful to your eyes and your inward parts, for the woods are full of evil spirits. We give you this string of wampum to clear up your eyes and minds and to remove all bitterness of your spirit, that you may hear us speak in good cheer.

Cousins and Nephews:

We formerly have faced each other as the bitterest of enemies. Today we have great joy that we can meet as relatives and friends. Because of this new relationship, we henceforth will greet the Lenape as "cousins" and the Mohicans as "nephews."

---

[40] Close to the present site of Albany, New York.

[41] The Dutch referred to the Mohicanichtuck as the North River. The English later called it the Hudson River.

[42] Held in the fall of 1621.

Cousins and Nephews:

We dress you in a woman's long habit, reaching down to your feet, and adorn you with earrings.

We hang a calabash filled with oil and medicine upon your arm. With the oil you shall cleanse the ears of the other nations that they may attend to good and not to bad words. With the medicine you shall heal those who are walking in foolish ways that they may return to their senses and incline their hearts to peace.

We deliver into your hands a plant of maize and a hoe.

Cousins and Nephews:

We, and everyone present, see that you have buried the tomahawk that you used against the Mengwe deep in the ground. We shall build a church over it. And if the Lenape or the Mohicans ever tear that church down and dig the tomahawk up again, the Dutch shall fall upon him and destroy him.

Cousins and Nephews:

We lay across the shoulders of the Lenni Lenape this peace belt. It shall be held up on the one end by the Mengwe and on the other end by the Europeans.

Narrated by Glikkikan

I still remember how Owechela stopped and laughed the day he taught me the lines about the Mengwe. Then with a twinkle in his eye he said, "Glikkikan, when two nations war, truth disappears in the shouts of battle. Both sides praise their own virtue; the enemy suffers the vilest passions.

"Glikkikan, when two men fight, they cannot see the right. Blinded by passion, they must both fight till they are knocked senseless. Only the kinder, gentler passions of the woman can reason with two crazed men and cause them to stop fighting.

"Glikkikan, it is the same when two nations fight. No matter how tired the two nations be of fighting, neither one dares be the coward and talk of peace. Men of honor must fight till they lie cold and still. For it is not proper to hold the peace belt in one hand and the tomahawk in the other. Men's words, as well as their actions, should be of one piece, all good or all bad; good can never dwell with evil. But if the tender and gentle woman comes forward and persuades the enraged combatants to bury their hatchets and make peace, both sides may be saved from the folly of fighting to the death, while the honor and the bravery of both nations remain intact."

"Owechela," I asked, "do you mean that the Lenape really did allow the Mengwe to trick them into becoming women?"

"Glikkikan, you must understand that it requires more courage to bow than to brawl. Tamenend would have approved of the Lenape being made women. Tamenend would have smiled that the Lenape, of their own free will, laid aside their weapons of war and dressed themselves in skirts reaching to the ground that they might become peacemakers. It was a role worthy of Tamenend's spirit."

"But Owechela, did you not teach me that the Mengwe lied, stole, killed, and did every other sort of evil? Did you not teach me that good and evil do not dwell in the same person? Did you not teach me that the Mengwe had been sly, cunning weasels for hundreds of years? Could the Mengwe suddenly turn inside out and become harmless, playful chipmunks?"

"Ah, Glikkikan, you learn your lessons well. I did teach you these things. But I did not yet teach you everything. Because you know a little, do not think you know it all. The quest for knowledge is like reaching for the end of the rainbow. The end always glows beyond us.

"Glikkikan, you have yet to learn that the worm can morph into the butterfly. You have yet to learn that no person or nation can bend the truth to fit around its own neck—neither the Lenape, the Mengwe, nor the Dutch. And you have yet to learn that the risk of failure calls forth the greatest need for courage.

"Glikkikan, you must learn that sometimes even your enemy speaks the truth. This time the Mengwe spoke the truth. Red men should not beat red men down and allow Schwanneks to pluck our red feathers until we all lie bare-skinned and singed before them.

"Glikkikan, listen well to the drama of the invasion of our Lenape homeland by the Schwanneks."

Eesanques and Bad Dog

As told by Owechela

The coming of the French, the Dutch, and the English
changed the whole world around for the Lenape.
Indeed, it changed the way of life for all the native
peoples, or what the Schwanneks call "Indians." I guess it's
no use to fight it any longer, so I, too, will call the native
peoples Indians when I'm referring to all the native tribes and
nations. It's just part of the overpowering changes that shake
the present.

So, as I was saying, instead of the Indians living off the
land and their own far-reaching trade networks as they had
for many centuries, in less than ten years the Indians became
hooked on European goods, which they could obtain only by
killing live animals to obtain their pelts. The rivalry among
the Europeans for the fur trade ensured that the depletion of
the beavers and other stock occurred over a wide area and not
just in one small locality.

However, it was not just the decreasing beaver supply and

the changing way of life for the Lenape that brought us into conflict with the Dutch. There were two more things.

The Dutch brought the Lenape brandy. It was never enough for the Lenape.

The Dutch bought more land. It was never enough for the Dutch.

And as at Drunk Island, when the Dutch bought land along the Lenape River, they meant for it to be only theirs. No one else, no Swedes, no English, and certainly NO "savages," as they called us, dare live there or use the land.

Of course the Lenape, as friends, allowed the white man to use the land as soon as he first came. When the Whites came to buy more land, we took them by the hand and bade them welcome. We told the Dutch and the Swedes and the English, "Come, sit down by our side and live with us as brothers."

And so it went when a Dutchman named Bad Dog Hossitt[43] came and wanted to "buy" land on both shores of the Lenape Bay where it meets the Salt Sea. Ten village chiefs of the area—Sawowouwe, Wuoyt, Pemhake, Mekowetick, Techepewoya, Mathemek, Sacook, Anehoopen, Janqueno, and Pokahake—made a peace pact[44] with the Dutch trading company Bad Dog Hossitt represented.

The Dutch "paid" for the land with trade goods—duffel cloth, axes, adzes, beads, needles—and the Lenape received those same "presents" given as a seal on the agreement just concluded.

The chiefs sent two of their older councilors, Eesanques and Quesquaekous, to represent them when the sale was

---

[43] Gillis Hossitt.

[44] The names of the chiefs taken from extant Dutch records. The "sale" took place June 1, 1629.

recorded[45] at Drunk Island. Turn Coat Minuit, the chief of the Dutch West India Company,[46] watched as Eesanques and Quesquaekous put their signs on the peace pact.

About a year after the land deals were concluded, Bad Dog Hossitt returned[47] with thirty-one Dutchmen to build a settlement at the point where the Siconece River enters the Lenape Bay. They named their planned village Swanendael.[48]

The first thing Bad Dog did upon his arrival was to erect a pole just outside the planned gate of the stockade. On that pole Bad Dog fastened a strange square piece of copper. Painted on the copper plate were two large tawny cats reared on their hind legs and facing each other. Between the two cats a third cat stood with a long drawn knife in one paw and a clutch of arrows in the other paw. Spread out over the top of the centerpiece was a strange gold hat.

"Do you pray to this sign? Is it the sign of your gods?" Eesanques asked of Bad Dog.

"It is the Arms of Holland," was all Bad Dog would tell Eesanques.

There the column and the pole stood as if to challenge the sea, the wilderness, and the Lenape as the thirty-two Dutchmen toiled to wrest from an alien land a New Netherland.

The settlers built a large dwelling house of yellow bricks brought from Holland and a cookhouse fitted with vats for boiling whale blubber. On the second floor of the main

---

[45] Recorded on the Island of Manhattan at Fort Amsterdam on July 11, 1630.

[46] Pieter Minuit (MIN-yew-ee). As head of the Dutch West India Company, he was also head of all Dutch interests in the New World.

[47] Settlers arrived on the ship *Walvis*, "Whale," in the spring of 1631.

[48] "Valley of Swans."

dwelling, the Dutchmen stored goods to be used in trade with the Lenape. Outside the door of the main building they chained a powerful crotch-high dog with hanging lips and drooping ears. They surrounded the whole area with palisades and mounted four great guns with their muzzles pointed toward the Lenape wigwams and fields outside the stakes.

The Dutchmen cared for the horses and cows they brought from Holland and prided themselves in the increase. The Dutch settlers planted tobacco and grain for export to Holland in the open fields "bought" from the Lenape.

Eesanques watched the Dutch planting in the Lenape fields and shook his head. Then he talked to Bad Dog Hossitt. "You cannot take our fields. We have always planted them. You must find other fields for your crops," he complained.

Bad Dog stood firm. "We bought this land from you. You are the ones who must leave and find other fields. If you do not get out and quit troubling us, we will destroy you, and then the fields will be ours for sure."

Eesanques went from one field to another. Patiently he warned the sweating settlers, "You must respect the Lenape claims on our homeland. We are going to continue to hunt and fish and farm the fields. We will stay here. You are the newcomers."

The longer Eesanques persisted in his talk, the more abusive Bad Dog became with him. Finally Hossitt cursed him saying, "Get out, you good-for-nothing, old, drunken, savage dog." The mastiff growled and leaped against his chain.

Eesanques brooded. At last he called together the chiefs who had sold the land—Sawowouwe, Wuoyt, Pemhake, Mekowetick, Techepewoya, Mathemek, Sacook, Anehoopen, Janqueno, and Pokahake. The warriors came with them to the council.

In the council hut they seated themselves around Eesanques in a quiet semicircle. The oldest ones in the first circle, the middle-aged in the second circle, and the youngest braves in the third circle. Patiently and quietly they waited for Eesanques to speak.

But instead of speaking, Eesanques removed the pipe hanging around his neck, took some tobacco from the pouch, placed it in the clay pipe bowl, and carefully lit it. He smoked briefly and then passed it around the circle from one chief to the next. When all had smoked, they returned the pipe to Eesanques. He carefully laid the pipe aside, allowing it to continue smoldering.

Next, Eesanques lifted from his arm a small white wampum belt with a copper heart in the center of it. He held it out for all to see.

Then he began. "Long ago the Eries gave this belt to the Lenape as proof of their friendship. Since that long-ago time it has been held out to the Cherokees as well as to other nations. The heart in the center is a heart of peace. As long as the heart does not change, the nations who have covenanted together with this belt shall be a people with one heart of love. As the ancient Erie orator exhorted us, we must examine the heart and see if it has changed."

Eesanques passed the belt to the nearest chief and queried, "Has the heart changed?" Eesanques resumed his seat and again puffed slowly on his pipe.

The chief inspected the belt minutely. Then he answered Eesanques's question by speaking to everyone and yet no one in particular, "The sinews of the belt show signs of wear, but the heart is true and unchanged." Then he passed the belt to the chief seated next to him for his inspection. And so the belt passed to the hand of each chief, and each chief concurred with the first chief's assessment, "The sinews of the belt show signs of wear, but the heart is true and unchanged."

After the belt had completed its round, Eesanques again laid it across his arm and declared, "The heart of the Lenape is true and unchanged. We are friends and of one heart with many people."

Finally, Eesanques rose to his feet and addressed the council:

> A long, long time ago, the Great Spirit gave us this land. It is our homeland.
>
> It is a good land of abundant food.
>
> From the streams we gather sturgeon larger than a grown man. In the shad moon we take the shad and other smaller fish in abundance. The seas also give up other delicacies—oysters, clams, crayfish, mussels, and scallops.
>
> We take the deer, bear, beaver, and otter in the chase. From them we gain not only food, but also soft skins and furs to keep us warm and clothed.
>
> The Great Spirit also sends to this good land herons, geese, ducks, and turkeys for us to eat; we also enjoy their beautiful plumage with its many uses.
>
> In the good soil we plant the squash, the beans, and the maize. And the manitos send rain. Not only do the gardens faithfully bring forth the staples of beans, squash, and maize, but the forest showers us with its delights—strawberries, blueberries, blackberries,

plums, apples, persimmons, walnuts, butternuts, hickory nuts, chestnuts, and acorns.

Ours is a good land. For hundreds of years we and our fathers and mothers have prospered here in the lands along the Siconece.

Do you wish to keep this good land? Look at the sky. Black clouds stalk the horizon, and they bring mighty winds that one day may drive us and our children forever from this place.

The clouds I speak of are three in number.

The first cloud is the cloud of sickness. It has been only twenty years since the Schwanneks showed their pale faces among us. The Schwanneks have cast powerful curses upon us, the spotted sicknesses, love sicknesses, and the fevers. Against these evils our medicine men seem powerless. They can find no roots or herbs or spells that prevent the sicknesses from killing us. The Lenape, and indeed all the red men, are greatly weakened by these sicknesses, which we never saw among us before the Schwanneks came.

The second cloud darkening the sky is brandy. The red man does not make firewater. Yes, as those of us know who were at Drunk Island, the sensations we enjoy from drinking the foul-smelling stuff astound us. But by drinking it we make fools of ourselves. We allow the trader to cheat us; we attack our friends; we experience fearful fancies; we destroy our own bodies and sometimes die. Indeed, we are selling our souls to the evil spirits in the rum until we care not for family, food, or race. We only thirst.

The third black cloud darkening the sun is the
Schwanneks' hunger for land. Only twenty years ago
the Schwanneks first appeared in our lands. The
Long Knives[49] came to the south of us and the Dutch
to the north of us.

They are different peoples, yet are they all the same.
All Schwanneks want to take our land from us. At
first they ask only for a little land on which to raise
bread for themselves and their families and pasture
for their cattle, which we freely give them. They soon
want more, which we also give them. They see the
game in the woods, which the Great Spirit has given
us for our sustenance, and they want that too. They
penetrate into the woods in quest of game; they
discover spots of land that please them; that land
they also want, and because we are loath to part with
it, as we see they already have more land than they
need, they take it from us by force and drive us a great
distance from our ancient homeland.

Do not let my words fall to the ground.

Here Eesanques stopped and sat down. Again the pipe
passed slowly from one chief to the other. At last it returned
to Eesanques. After a long smoke, he laid the pipe aside and
stood before the council once more. He spoke slowly with
lengthy pauses between his thoughts.

I have been to Drunk Island. I was there when the
Schwanneks first came. I have returned to confirm
the purchase of the land you agreed to let them have
at the place they call Swanendael.

[49] The Indians called the English from Virginia "Long Knives" because of their swords.

All is not well at Drunk Island. More and more Schwanneks crowd in upon our red brethren.

The game is gone from the fields.

The Indian dogs worry the poultry and livestock of the Schwanneks. The Schwanneks shoot the dogs.

The cows, goats, and pigs of the Schwanneks run unattended through the Indian fields. The Indians dare do nothing or they themselves will be thrown in jail or worse.

And often it is worse.

When the red man resists, the Dutch shoot him.

Now, look at our own homeland. The Schwanneks are here.

Even now they plant our fields. They hunt our game in the forests. They take our fish from the streams.

They build houses for women and children, and those houses are not for our women and children. They build forts to protect themselves from whom if not from us?

Do the Schwanneks plant great guns to use against bears and panthers if perchance they should attack the fort? No, they plant great guns to use against us.

Do you wish to be driven from your homeland? Do you want to be shot down like dogs when the Schwanneks become strong?

Already they abuse us, calling us dogs and savages. They molest our women.

We have but one choice if we would avoid being destroyed by the coming storm.

We must strike them down now. All thirty-two
Schwanneks in this place must be slain. Not one of
them dare escape to tell the tale.

The words of Eesanques are ended.

Probably no one would ever have acted on Eesanques's
counsel. The Lenape were not organized into united warring
parties. And to kill strangers to whom they had promised
the use of their lands was alien to their very nature. Probably
Eesanques's warning of a coming clash with the Schwanneks
and expulsion from our homeland along the Lenape River
and Lenape Bay would have fallen to the ground except for
what happened next.

Eesanques got drunk ... again. In his drunken stupor he
staggered to the column at the gate of the stockade and
tore from it the piece of copper adorned with the Arms of
Holland. Eesanques threw the hated symbol to the ground,
placed both feet upon it, and raised his tomahawk toward the
sky.

In that defiant state, Bad Dog, stationed at the gate, shot
Eesanques dead. As he crumpled, his blood pooled out over
the copper sign.

The Lenape came, quietly gathered up Eesanques and buried
him with his tomahawk in his hand and the copper sign beneath
his feet. No one seemed to notice, but someone had cut a palm-
sized square out of one corner of the hated sign.

Then one fine spring day, when thirty of the Dutch settlers
were working in the fields, the Lenape returned to the

stockade. They killed Bad Dog Hossitt at the gate. Another man too sick to work they killed in his bed. Warriors shot twenty-four arrows through the mastiff. One by one they murdered all thirty of the other men in the fields. Not one Dutchman was left to tell the tale. They killed the horses, the cows, and the calves. Then they burned the stockade and destroyed the buildings.

After the last embers of Swanendael died out, quiet reigned along the River of the Lenape for six years. Only an occasional trading vessel sailed up the Lenape River and traded goods for furs. The Lenape noted in sullen silence the Dutch flag—top stripe red, middle stripe white, bottom stripe dark blue—hung from the topmast of each ship.

Uneasy Lenape paddled up and down the river in their dugouts, gathering at council fires and pondering the last words of Eesanques. Surely the Dutch would avenge the death of their brethren, and it was better that the Lenape be prepared to strike back as one arm.

In this anxious state of mind the Lenape waited.

Narrated by Glikkikan

Owechela stopped. He seemed to be thinking whether he should say something else or not. He studied me a while, then decided to go on.

"Glikkikan, when we search for the truth in life, we must never be still. We must never stop looking ... and thinking.

"Perhaps we know nothing about Swanendael. Perhaps we do not want to know. Then we are willingly ignorant.

"Perhaps we do not understand everything we know about Swanendael. Someday understanding may come.

"Perhaps we do not yet know everything about Swanendael. If we know that we do *not* know, we will seek the truth.

"Perhaps we think we know the truth about Swanendael when we do not. That is the most dangerous condition of all, for men lock what they surely know in their hearts, and neither thunder nor lightning can show them the truth.

"Glikkikan, we do not need to fear examining the truth. Truth is like a piece of gold that may be taken from our bosom and admired. If we polish it a bit as we hold it, it will only shine all the brighter.

"Glikkikan, because of the story I have taught you about Swanendael, you think you know the truth about what happened there. You think you know why the Lenape killed the Dutch. I believe what you know is true. But there is more than what I have told you, perhaps more than you can understand now, but I think I should tell you some now, and you will understand better when you become a man.

"Glikkikan, when the Great Spirit made men and women, he made them different than the animals. Most animals and birds mate with any partner they can find. However, men and women are like eagles that mate for life, and always with the same partner. The Great Spirit made us that way.

"Glikkikan, when the Dutch first came to the Siconece River, years before the building of Swanendael, the Lenape opened up their wigwams to their guests and shared everything they had, their food, beds, and, on occasion, the

The Swanendael Massacre

Lenape allowed their guests to sleep with their wives and their daughters. Many Dutchmen were far from home, and after long sea voyages gladly bought the favors of the Lenape women. The practice became so common that the Dutch named the place, Whore's Creek.[50] A whore is a woman, who contrary to her nature, and like the animals, sleeps with many different men.

"Glikkikan, when thirty-two Dutchmen came to Swanendael, they were a long way from home and very lonely. Perhaps they sought the companionship and favors of the Lenape women. Perhaps they demanded those favors and even forced their advances on the Lenape women. Eesanques hinted at such when he said, 'They molest our women.'

"Glikkikan, have you ever watched two stags fight over the favors of a doe? It is much worse when the rage of a husband burns against another man who has stolen the favors of his wife. Nothing can appease his wrath. Such a husband or forsaken lover will kill his rival or kill himself trying.

"Glikkikan, perhaps the Swanendael killings had more to do with jealous and enraged men than it had to do with a pole and a piece of copper. Today there are few Lenape left anywhere near the site of Swanendael, but for a while blue-eyed and lighter-skinned Lenape sometimes lived in the nearby villages. Ponder what I have told you. Someday, when you are ready to receive it, I will tell you more of the mystery of Swanendael."

[50] The Hoerenkill.

Mattahorn and Turn Coat

As told by Owechela

To the surprise of the anxious Lenape, no one showed up to punish them. Instead, two ships pushed their way up the Lenape River bearing strange flags on their topmasts. These flags bore a blue background with two crossed yellow bars on them.

The captain of the ships was none other than the Dutchman Turn Coat Minuit,[51] the former head of the Dutch West India Company who at Drunk Island had recorded the earlier purchases of the Swanendael land. When the two ships reached the mouth of Minqua Creek[52] that emptied into the Lenape River from the west, they turned and followed it upstream to "The Rocks," where they were well hidden from the main river. There Minuit fired his great guns two times; then he went ashore to look around.

When Turn Coat Minuit returned to the ships, he found that the roar of the cannon had brought the desired effect.

[51] Pronounced "MIN-yew-wee."

[52] The Susquehannocks, or Minquas, used this as a trade route to the Delaware River.

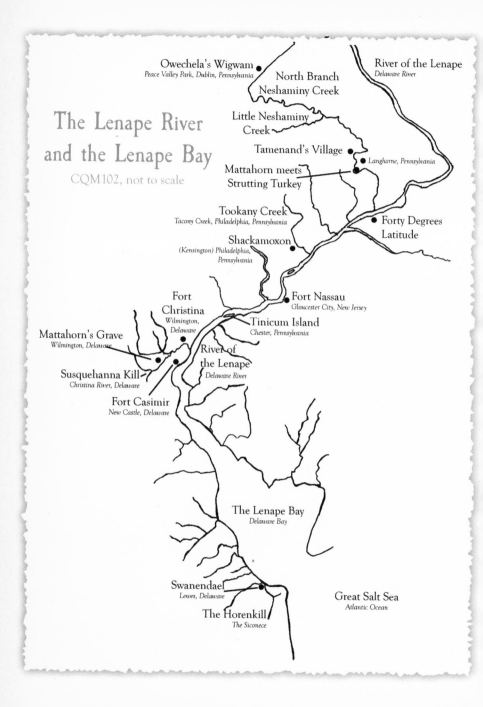

Owechela's Wigwam
Peace Valley Park, Dublin, Pennsylvania

North Branch
Neshaminy Creek

River of the Lenape
Delaware River

The Lenape River
and the Lenape Bay
CQM102, not to scale

Little Neshaminy
Creek

Tamenand's Village

Langhorne, Pennsylvania

Mattahorn meets
Strutting Turkey

Tookany Creek
Tacony Creek, Philadelphia, Pennsylvania

Forty Degrees
Latitude

Shackamoxon
*(Kensington) Philadelphia,
Pennsylvania*

Fort
Christina
*Wilmington,
Delaware*

Fort Nassau
Gloucester City, New Jersey

Tinicum Island
Chester, Pennsylvania

Mattahorn's Grave
Wilmington, Delaware

River of
the Lenape
Delaware River

Susquehanna Kill
Christina River, Delaware

Fort Casimir
New Castle, Delaware

The Lenape Bay
Delaware Bay

Swanendael
Lewes, Delaware

Great Salt Sea
Atlantic Ocean

The Horenkill
The Siconece

Mattahorn and four other Lenape chiefs were waiting on him when he returned.

Turn Coat greeted Mattahorn warmly. "I have heard much of you from former days, and I am happy that I found you so quickly."

"And I have heard that at Drunk Island you bought many skins," Mattahorn replied evasively. Then Mattahorn asked boldly, "Why do you come here now? Why the two ships and the great guns? Have you come to kill us?"

"No, no," Turn Coat Minuit assured the suspicious Lenape. "I have not come to punish you. I have nothing to do anymore with the Dutch at Drunk Island or the Dutch West India Company. See," he said, pointing to the flag at the top of his ship, "I now come from a different country called Sweden. These ships, the *Kalmar Nyckel*[53] and the *Grip*, have been sent out by a beautiful young queen named Christina. The Swedes are true Christians and just in their dealings.

"If you will trade with us, we will give you a much better deal than the stingy Dutch.

"Look," Turn Coat continued, "I have on these ships several thousand yards of duffels and other cloth; several hundred axes, hatchets, adzes, and knives; dozens of tobacco pipes; mirrors, looking glasses, gilded chains, finger rings, combs, and earrings. Will you trade with me?"

"Why should I think that you will treat us any differently now than you did when you were chief at Drunk Island?" Mattahorn quizzed.

"Listen to me," Turn Coat urged. "If you will sell me ground on which to build a house, I will give you a kettle,

---

[53] The *Kalmar Nyckel* (Key of Calmar). The *Kalmar Nyckel* Foundation maintains a re-creation of this ship and schedules regular sails open to the public. Contact <www.kalmarnyckel.org> Wilmington, Delaware.

duffel cloth, an ax, a tobacco pipe, a looking glass, and earrings. If you will sell me ground on which to plant crops, I will give you half the tobacco raised upon it."

"Where do you want your plantation?" probed Mattahorn.

Turn Coat was ready. He led Mattahorn and the others on a slow walk to a nice gentle rise some distance from the river. As they walked along, Turn Coat pointed out six trees that formed a rough border around a field. Mattahorn said nothing. His face betrayed not a sign of emotion as he neatly notched a turtle on the bark of each of the six trees.

At the conclusion of the walk, Mattahorn said to Minuit, "We will bring you an answer tomorrow after we build our council fire. It is not our custom to give an answer quickly."

So it came about that in the shad moon five Lenape sachems—Mattahorn, Mitatsemint, Elupacken, Mahamen, and Chiton—boarded the Kalmar Nyckel. Chiefs from other nations, including the powerful Susquehannocks to the west, accompanied them on board.

Mattahorn spoke for the Lenape chiefs.

> Friend, you have come a long way to visit us. You have asked us to sell you ground. We have met by the council fire. The field you have asked for is a large one. But other things concern us more than the amount of the ground you have asked to buy from us.
>
> Friend, you well know how the Dutch treated our brothers at Drunk Island. First they asked for only a little ground to build a house on or to set a chair on. Soon that was not enough. More Schwanneks came. The Schwanneks wanted more ground. They wanted not only the empty ground, but even the ground the natives planted. If our grandchildren, the Mohicans,

would not give it to them, the Schwanneks took it anyway. Is not this true?

Friend, is it not true that you yourself bought the whole island of Manahachtánienk for the Dutch? Is it not true that even now the Dutch kill the Lenape and the Mohicans and sell them as slaves if they will not leave it all to the Schwanneks?

Friend, I am sure you know of the Dutch settlement at Swanendael. I am sure you know Bad Dog and his men intended to do the same at that place as they did at Drunk Island. And it is likely that you even approved of what they did. But those settlers all died.

Friend, let it be known to you that the Lenape do not want to leave their homeland. The Great Spirit has given us this land, and we have lived here for hundreds and hundreds of years. It is the Land of the Lenape, and we will keep it.

Friend, we are fearful of the Dutch. They have many strong inventions that we marvel at—paper talk, axes, cloth, wheels, ships, guns, and great guns. But they also have brandy. And the Dutch will lie and steal and cheat and kill if they can gain from it. We are afraid of them.

Friend, if you will raise your arm to protect us from the Dutch, you may have ground on which to build a house. You may use the ground to grow crops upon, and one-half of any tobacco you grow will be ours. We will continue to hunt in the forests and fish in the streams of our homeland as we always have.

Friend, come live among us and we will dwell together in peace.

Turn Coat Minuit waited no longer. He brought out the promised kettle. He made small piles of trade goods on the floor for each of the Lenape sachems. On top of each pile he laid one bright red blanket. Four thumb-wide black stripes sewn the full width of the blanket adorned each end of the blanket. Black-threaded blanket stitches graced the edges.

"Now," Turn Coat continued, "all can see that we have treated you kindly. The hold of the ship still bears much goods of the same kind. If you will bring us your beaver pelts, otter skins, and bearskins, we will treat you with the same kindness as we have shown here today.

"There is still one item we must attend to today. Good Queen Christina has done her part. Now the Lenape must do theirs. I have prepared on paper a record of the land you have sold us. Here is what I have written:

> On this the 29th day of March 1638, five Lenape
> sachems—Mattahorn, Mitatsemint, Elupacken,
> Mahamen, and Chiton—have ceded, transported, and
> transferred the land to Queen Christina for as many
> days' journey as we wish on all places and parts of the
> river known to them as the Lenape River upwards
> and on both sides of the river. For this land the
> Indians were paid and fully compensated by good and
> proper merchandise, which was delivered and given to
> them in the personal presence of witnesses from the
> Susquehannock nation.[54]

"At this time," Turn Coat continued, "you five sachems shall draw your totem at the bottom of the parchment. I and

---

[54] The original document was lost at sea. This recreated document is based on an affidavit by surviving crew members. —*The Delaware Indians*, Weslager, p. 118.

my partner will put our marks with yours. Then Christina will know what we have done here today in her name."

After fixing their marks to the parchment, the Lenape and the other chiefs gathered up their gifts, left the ship, and quickly reunited with their assembled friends and families on shore.

But the natives were not alone. They watched at close range as Turn Coat Minuit, his officers, and his soldiers joined them on the shore. The group marched solemnly past them to the nearby field marked by the six oak trees.

On a slight rise Turn Coat and his party planted a pole. Hanging from the pole was a two-foot-square piece of tin. Painted on the tin in a field of blue were three golden hats. Gold leaves trimmed the outside border of the tin, and another large hat interspersed with red stones formed the top.

Turn Coat's group stood stiffly and quietly in front of the pole while Turn Coat and several of the other leaders made long speeches. At times, the men removed their hats. At last they fired the great guns on the ships and then everyone shouted.

Mattahorn watched it all. He wondered, "What kind of idols are these that the Schwanneks worship? Do the Schwanneks not know the Great Spirit? And why do the Schwanneks carry guns and long knives, and why do they shoot the great guns?"

Again, Mattahorn remembered the words of Eesanques: "Do the Schwanneks plant great guns to use against bears and panthers if perchance they should attack the fort? No, they plant great guns to use against us."

Mattahorn's stomach turned uneasily as if he had eaten unroasted acorns. *Can the Lenape live peaceably with the*

Schwanneks, or was Eesanques right? he wondered. *Will they indeed drive us from our homeland?*

Uneasily, Mattahorn questioned Turn Coat. "What did you and your soldiers do today?" he asked.

Turn Coat Minuit explained: "We named the land we bought from you New Sweden. And we named the creek the Christina in honor of the queen who bought the land. And we named the fort we are going to build here by the water's edge Fort Christina."

Fort Christina soon started taking shape close by the mysterious pole. Swedish settlers nursed blisters that soon hardened into calluses while they toiled to build homes and a fort in the wilds of New Sweden. And they planted great guns in the fort pointed not at the river, but well aimed at the surrounding wilderness.

Turn Coat waited. And he waited. No Lenape showed up bringing furs to trade. A month passed. Finally he made his way to Mattahorn's wigwam. Mattahorn fed him. They smoked the pipe for a long time.

Finally Mattahorn spoke. "Captain Minuit," he said softly, "what errand brings you to my wigwam?"

"Sachem Mattahorn," he replied, "when you came on board the *Kalmar Nyckel,* I showed you many goods. I did not bring these goods here to eat nor to give out as gifts. I want to trade them for furs and skins. I will give more goods for them than the Dutch. Why do the Lenape not bring me their furs and skins?"

"Captain Minuit, I would ask a question of you. When you were the Great Sachem at Manahachtánienk, how many beaver pelts did you buy and send to Holland?"

"During the six years I was in charge of the West India

Company at Manahachtánienk we sent 47,196 beaver skins and 5,388 otter skins to Holland."

"Captain Minuit, you bought many, many pelts. You did very well for the Dutch. Now tell me, did you leave Drunk Island and the Dutch West India Company because you wanted to pay the Indians more for their pelts? And from whom did you buy all these pelts?"

"Sachem Mattahorn, I did not exactly leave the Dutch West India Company because I wanted to. The company suspected I was not doing things properly. But back to your question: I bought pelts from the Mengwe, the Susquehannocks, the Lenape, and the Mohicans. And a lot of them came from the region of the Lenape River. By setting up our trading post here, we are trying to make it easier for the Lenape to get their pelts to us."

"Captain Minuit," said Mattahorn, going for the jugular, "when you were the Great Sachem, did all of your traders deal fairly and honestly? Did YOU always deal fairly and honestly? How do we know that the snake has not just shed its red, white, and blue skin only to grow a new skin of bluish-green and yellow?"

Turn Coat Minuit hung his head. He knew only too well the "tricks of the trade"—tightly cupping the hand when measuring out Indian meal, buying when the customer was drunk, adding water to the brandy. "Sachem Mattahorn," he said, "you are wise. You know that evil spirits do torment me. But I can promise you that I will not sell brandy to the Lenape. Try me and see if I do not trade fairly, honestly, and more generously than the Dutch."

At first, the Lenape timidly brought a few skins to Turn Coat. They soon found he did indeed give them more goods for their skins and pelts than the Dutch. Then the skins and pelts really piled in to the new trading post of Fort Christina. Even the Susquehannocks from the river to the west brought a few pelts.

Before Turn Coat Minuit sailed off, he returned once more to Mattahorn's wigwam to thank him for his help. Captain Minuit reported to Sachem Mattahorn that he carried on his ships 1,769 beaver pelts, 314 otter skins, and 132 bearskins. He was sure the New Sweden Company would be pleased.

The spring following Turn Coat's departure from Christina, a new head for the colony arrived, Peter Hollender Ridder. Not long after his arrival, Governor Peter Ridder made the short trip to Mattahorn's wigwam.

"Sachem Mattahorn," he said, "I understand that you sold Captain Minuit the land where Christina now stands. Is that right?"

"I did not sell it to him by myself. I and four other Lenape sachems sold Captain Minuit only enough ground to build his house on. We agreed to let him have ground to plant his crops on. That ground is clearly marked by a turtle carved

The Kalmar Nyckel returns to the River of the Lenape.

CQ106

in the trunk of each of the six trees at the border of the field surrounding Christina."

"Then will you and the other sachems again put your totems on the paper to show Queen Christina the sale indeed took place?" Governor Ridder asked.

Mattahorn lit his pipe and smoked in silence for some time. Then he asked, "Governor Ridder, what has happened to the parchment that we already put our totems on?"

"It is gone with Captain Minuit," sighed Governor Ridder.[55]

"Governor Ridder," said Mattahorn, choosing his words carefully, "you must understand that the paper is gone. Our memory endures if the paper does not. We do not know what the paper spoke, but we know well what we spoke to Captain Minuit. Our meaning is as plain as the sun. As long as the Swedes protect us from the Dutch and live peaceably among us, the Swedes may remain in the Land of the Lenape.

"You do not need paper to write that on, and we will not again put our totems on something that has already been settled. Clean out your ears. I do not speak to you with a forked tongue. You have not bought our homeland that you may drive us away."

Governor Peter Hollender Ridder understood.

He found two Lenape sachems named Kekesikkun and Shakapemeck. Kekesikkun and Shakapemeck "sold" Ridder land on both sides of the river as far as fifty miles north of Christina. And for adequate presents spiced with brandy and rum, they gladly drew their totems on any piece of paper

---

[55] When Captain Minuit left the *Fogel Grip* at Christina, he sailed on the *Kalmar Nyckel* to the Island of St. Christopher in the Caribbean and exchanged his skins and pelts for tobacco. While there in the harbor, he and his ship captain (van der Water) were visiting on board another ship, *de Vliegende Hart* (the "Flying Hart"), when a sudden storm drove all twenty ships in the harbor about one-half hour out to sea. The *Kalmar Nyckel* survived and returned with its cargo to Holland and then Sweden. The *Vliegende Hart* along with Peter Minuit and his ship captain perished in the storm.

Ridder held before them.

Five years went by while the little colony at Fort Christina grew. Scattered hamlets spread out along the Christina. The Lenape continued favoring the Swedes over the Dutch by bringing their furs and skins to the little trading post. More and more of the Susquehannocks came from the west and brought their skins down Minqua Creek to Fort Christina. The trading post at Christina struggled to handle the volume.

A new sachem came to Christina.

From his wigwam near Christina, Mattahorn heard that the new sachem of the Swedes wanted yet more furs. In fact, Mattahorn gathered, the new sachem wanted ALL the furs from the Valley of the Lenape and even those from the much greater Valley of the Susquehannocks to the west. To that end, the new sachem began yet another Swedish settlement on Tinicum Island in the Lenape River due east from a Swedish settlement on the west bank of the river.[56]

Mattahorn and five warriors paddled their dugout the fifteen miles up the Lenape River several times to study the settlement. Each time they swung lazily around the island and then drifted steadily homeward.

On the first trip during the harvest moon,[57] Mattahorn could easily pick out the pole with its sacred green and yellow tin hanging on it. He noted the outline of the fort.

On subsequent journeys Mattahorn watched the village grow. The walls of the fort, built of green hemlock logs cut

[56] Settlement at present Chester, Pennsylvania.
[57] The month of October when the maize is harvested.

and stacked one upon another, gradually rose higher and higher until a warrior could not touch the top of them with his arm extended. Central to the fort rose a new two-story log house for the sachem. All buildings stood in neat rows within the fort. One dock large enough to accommodate sailing ships nestled along one side. Docks for smaller boats joined the larger docks. Just within the fort several large sheds housed the skins and furs. And at this fort the great guns pointed toward the Lenape River.

On his trip up the Lenape River during the fawn moon[58] to study the fort once more, Mattahorn determined that all was ready. Small boats brought furs and skins to the island as Swedish traders gathered them in from their trips up and down the streams flowing into the Lenape River. A large sailing vessel with its flag of blue background and yellow crossbars floated quietly by the dock. Soldiers manned the gates and stood in readiness. Workers hurried about, loading and unloading boats. Over it all stood the imposing energy of a strong sachem in a log mansion in the center of the fort. Directly west across the river from the new fort a normal Swedish village bustled about the business of living as it supported the business going on at the island.

When his canoe reached home, Mattahorn picked up a string of fifteen wampum beads. Holding it in his outstretched right hand, he addressed one of the warriors who accompanied him. As Mattahorn recited each segment of the message, he pushed one wampum bead forward on the string.

This is the message you shall bear to the
Great Sachem of the Swedes on Tinicum Island:

[58] The month of June when the deer give birth.

"Mattahorn, the Great Sachem of the Lenape, and four other Lenape sachems will meet with him in ten days when the summer moon is full. We will be at his house when the sun stands straight overhead. The five Lenape sachems who will come are the same five Lenape sachems who treated with Captain Minuit—Mattahorn, Mitatsemint, Elupacken, Mahamen, and Chiton."

Mattahorn handed the string of white wampum to the warrior. The warrior held the wampum reverently in his outstretched right hand, and looking straight into Mattahorn's eyes he repeated, "This is the message of the wampum that I will bear to the Great Sachem of the Swedes." The warrior thumbed one bead forward and then continued, "Mattahorn, the Great Sachem of the Lenape, and four other Lenape sachems will meet with him in ten days when the summer moon is full. The sachems will be at his house when the sun stands straight overhead. The five Lenape sachems who will come are the same five Lenape sachems who treated with Captain Minuit—Mattahorn, Mitatsemint, Elupacken, Mahamen, and Chiton." As he repeated the name "Chiton," the warrior thumbed the last of the fifteen wampum beads forward.

"Go in peace," Mattahorn commanded.

Without another word the warrior turned and set off alone through the woods to carry out his sacred duty. In his extended hand he held the string of white wampum that friend and foe alike might see he was a message bearer. The warrior knew that no red man would touch him while he carried that string of wampum.

Dusk was falling when the lone warrior arrived at the fort. The guard stopped him. He studied the warrior at the gate. The warrior carried no tomahawk, bow, or knife. He held only the string of wampum in his hand and waited motionless before him. The warrior's eyes held a faraway look as though it would take great effort to come back to the fort and the guard standing in his way. He did not appear to have been drinking.

What should he do? the guard wondered. Should he allow the warrior to enter at this hour? Should he sound the alarm? Should he try to find an interpreter? "Oh, well. Why bother?" he muttered. "Let the crazy Indian sleep outside." The guard closed the gate for the night.

At dawn the warrior still stood motionless outside the gate holding the wampum in his outstretched hand. The guard on duty sent for an interpreter.

"What do you want?" the guard asked.

"I bear a message for the Great Sachem of the Swedes," the warrior replied.

"And is the message urgent?" queried the guard.

"It is," responded the warrior.

The guard sent for another soldier of some authority. "This Indian bears an urgent message for Governor Printz," the guard told him. "He has been waiting all night at the gate."

"You stupid guards," grumbled the soldier. "Could you not see the wampum the warrior carries? You must be blind in one eye and can't see out of the other." And then to the warrior, "Come, I will take you to the Great Sachem. He is an early riser and will no doubt be anxious to receive your message."

Governor Printz himself met the three of them—the warrior, the soldier, and the interpreter—at the door. The governor flung the door open and filled the whole doorway with his presence. His beady eyes focused on the three standing on the ground below him. He noted the wampum in the warrior's hand.

Printz quickly stepped down to ground level where he still towered over the others. "I will receive the message you have for me," he told the warrior.

"Are you the Great Sachem of the Swedes?" the warrior asked.

"I am the Great Sachem of the Swedes," Printz boomed.

"Then this is the message of the wampum that I bear to the Great Sachem of the Swedes." The warrior thumbed the first bead forward and then continued, "Mattahorn, the Great Sachem of the Lenape, and four other Lenape sachems will meet with him in ten days when the summer moon is full. The sachems will be at his house when the sun stands straight overhead. The five Lenape sachems who will come are the same five Lenape sachems who treated with Captain Minuit— Mattahorn, Mitatsemint, Elupacken, Mahamen, and Chiton." As he finished, the warrior pushed the last of the beads forward and then held the wampum out to the Great Sachem.

Governor Printz reached out his hand and picked up the proffered wampum. "I accept. Let me get a quill and ink so that I may write the message down properly." Governor Printz jotted down the names of the sachems and the exact time of the proposed meeting. He verified them with the warrior.

"Now," he said to the warrior, "tell the Great Sachem Mattahorn that I accept. All will be in readiness."

"Soldier," Printz commanded next, "feed this poor savage well. Then carry him to the rogue Mattahorn in my personal boat."

The interpreter didn't get the last command exactly right.

He rendered it to the warrior, "Go with the soldier now and he will return you to the Great Sachem Mattahorn."

But the warrior understood anyway. "Rogue! Savage!" He had heard those words many times before.

Narrated by Glikkikan

"Owechela, what is the difference between the Dutch and the Swedes?" I asked. "Was Turn Coat really a bad man for switching from the Dutch to the Swedes?"

Owechela laughed. "Ho! Ho! Glikkikan. If you think Turn Coat was a puzzle, wait till you hear the story of Big Belly, the immense governor of New Sweden. Try to figure him out."

Chapter 6 — 1643-1653

Mattahorn and Big Belly

As told by Owechela

The great day agreed upon arrived. True to his word,
Sachem Printz had everything in readiness. As the boats
carrying the sachems touched the dock of the fort, the
great guns boomed out a salute.

This trip, soldiers carrying a small Swedish flag promptly
escorted all guests from the docks to the area just outside
Printz's mansion.

Outside under two trees, two great kettles steamed with
mush made from maize and wheat called *sappan*. Berries,
squash, and venison waited in readiness.

When the sun stood straight overhead, Governor Printz
welcomed all the guests to Tinicum. "This day is a special
day for us to meet as friends. We know that you have made
a long journey. You should rest and refresh yourselves before
we begin our work. We have prepared for you some of the
goodness from the land. This is a good land the Almighty
God has given us, and we want to thank Him for His
goodness today. When I came to New Sweden, a very special

assistant came on the ship with me, the Reverend John Campanius. He is a minister of the God that all the Christian nations serve. Part of his work here is to teach the natives about this God. I present him to you as Pastor Campanius. Pastor Campanius will now offer a prayer of thanksgiving for this meal."

And to the huge surprise and pleasure of every guest, John Campanius offered a short but simple prayer in the Lenape tongue.

> *Our Father who is in the sky, we thank your great name.*
> *Give us this day a plentiful supply of venison and maize.*
> *Forgive us today as we forgive those who wrong us.*
> *Save us from evil spirits.*
> *You, Father, will rule the earth and the sky forever.*
> *Ah-men.*

No one was sure exactly how it happened, but as soon as Pastor Campanius offered the "Ah-men," Swedes and Lenape together cried, "Ah-men! Ah-men!"

After the stirring prayer, the Lenape sachems moved forward and picked out their food first, then seated themselves in a small circle on the ground. After the sachems were seated, the other natives went forward, dished out their food, and then seated themselves on the ground in small circles removed from the sachems. Everyone ate till all were satisfied.

The five sachems cut a striking figure. Perfectly accenting his shoulder-length jet-black hair and dark eyes, each sachem wore a bright red blanket draped over his left shoulder and flung back around to the front underneath his right arm. A black silk scarf fit trimly around each neck, pinned together by a gold clasp with the loose ends of the scarf dangling over the chest. Buckskin breeches and soft moccasins covered their legs and feet from the waist down while their ears, bared arms, and bared chests flashed with bracelets, pendants, and earrings. Dangling from a wide belt, but mostly hidden by the blanket, each sachem carried a short-handled small ax and a sheathed knife.

Of the five Lenape sachems, Mattahorn alone bore a special mark. Tattooed on his bared right chest, the image of a turtle with twelve segments marked on its carapace crawled diagonally upward toward his left shoulder.

When the sachems had eaten and properly rested, a soldier escorted the sachems into the council room on the lower floor of Printz's mansion. The soldier pointed to the wood floor in front of a large empty chair waiting at the front of the room. The sachems quietly seated themselves on the floor in a semicircle fifteen feet back from the great chair. Mattahorn took his place with two sachems on either side.

Mattahorn looked about the room. A lone Swede stood beside the great chair. A secretary sat to one side at a table, ready to record the business, while Pastor Campanius and several other officials had seated themselves on a long bench opposite the secretary's table. Two soldiers stood guard at the door.

One of the officials on the bench stood up and announced, "In honor of Her Majesty, Queen Christina, and of her appointed governor of New Sweden, Johan Printz, will everyone please stand."

The man standing beside the great chair translated the announcement into Lenape. Five sachems rose to their feet along with the Swedes. Then the door opened and in strode Governor Johan Printz. Even a floor-length black robe could not hide his military bearing nor silence his commanding presence. Governor Printz gave a slight bow to the sachems and seated himself in the great chair. All in the room again took seats except the soldiers and the interpreter.

Mattahorn studied the governor closely as he seated himself. Governor Printz raised a large rough hand to his neck and carefully adjusted the white napkin attached to his collar. He smoothed the folds of his robes, allowing his wide lace cuffs to flare conspicuously across the black robe. He shifted his large head twice to adjust his long brown hair that flowed down onto his shoulders. He rubbed his right forefinger across the patch of short hair covering his upper lip. Printz was a big man. But it was his darting, beady eyes that fascinated Mattahorn. Could he trust this man?

Without rising from his great chair, Governor Printz began the meeting. "Sachem Mattahorn, Sachem Mitatsemint, Sachem Elupacken, Sachem Mahamen, and Sachem Chiton," he boomed. "Welcome to Tinicum Island. You have requested a meeting with me. I do not yet know the nature of your business, but I think it in order for me to tell you first some of what is happening in New Sweden. When the ships *Fame* and *Swan* brought Pastor Campanius, myself, and other Swedish settlers to New Sweden just over a year ago, we found several thriving settlements. But there were some problems.

"The Dutch are very jealous of any peltries the Swedes buy from the Lenape and the Susquehannocks. From the time of Captain Minuit's voyage until today, the Dutch have continually protested our presence on the Lenape River. The present Dutch Governor Kieft at New Amsterdam is a madman, and as soon as he thinks he is strong enough, he will use bullets instead of words to try to force New Sweden to submit to him. If he succeeds in conquering New Sweden, all the fur trade shall then belong to the Dutch.

"However, the Swedes are not weaklings. Our armies are strong. Our factories make many of the great guns for European armies. I have commanded large armies in Europe. I shall close the Lenape River to the ships and the settlements of the Dutch. Let the Dutch keep the North River for themselves, but we shall keep the South River[59] for the Swedes." No one in the room doubted Governor Printz meant to keep his word. Then he went on.

"I was not in New Sweden long before I discovered an ongoing dispute over the ownership of the land on which our villages are set. Some of you," and here he bored those beady eyes straight at Mattahorn, "claim that you have not sold the land to us, even though we have deeds to prove it. I have looked into the matter."

Governor Printz leaned forward in his chair. "You yourselves and other proper owners have received 'good and merchantable merchandise' as payment for the land you sold 'up and down the river, and on both sides.' The blankets you are wearing bear testimony that this is true. All the land on which our settlements grow, and indeed the land on this island has been justly bought and paid for. By contesting the deeds we hold, you only hope to receive more goods from us as bounty."

And then with an air of authority such as makes soldiers march forward to their death, Governor Printz continued, "We will not buy the land from you more than once."

Five sachems did not flinch. Not one eye twitched. Ten eyes stayed locked on those beady, shifting eyes. With the patience of the hunter trained by long hours of remaining motionless while the prey approached, they waited. The beady eyes shifted to the floor, and Governor Printz eased back slightly

[59] The Dutch referred to the Hudson River as the North River and the Delaware River as the South River.

on his chair.

Governor Printz went on. "Another problem I discovered soon after coming was that the trading post at Christina could not handle the large volume of trade goods and supplies New Sweden needs or the large number of peltries being gathered for transport to Europe. It seemed obvious to me, a former general, that we could not defend the trading post at Christina against possible attacks by natives or the Dutch. My solution was to build a strong fortress here on Tinicum Island where we could secure the supplies coming to the settlers, the trade goods for the fur trade, and the furs and skins leaving the country.

"As you can see for yourselves, we now have this post well established and protected. We are already receiving many furs and skins from the traders fanning out to the west. But I want more. The furs we now receive do not pay the cost of supporting the settlements and the government of New Sweden. Unless we can obtain more furs and skins, we shall be abandoned by Sweden.

"During my first year as governor, I found out that most of the furs coming here arrive from the Susquehannocks to the west. The Lenape sell us only a few furs and lots of maize. The settlers need the maize, but why do the Lenape not sell us more furs?

"Perhaps we do not need the Lenape," Printz threatened. "If the Lenape were gone, we could grow all the maize we need ourselves. A couple hundred soldiers could easily break the necks of all the Lenape on this river."[60]

At this bold pronouncement Mattahorn remained perfectly still. Not one muscle in his body twitched. But out of the corner of his eye he saw Pastor Campanius squirm. The

[60] An actual quote from one of governor Printz's reports.

preacher's mouth fell open, but he said nothing.

Without any hesitation Governor Printz continued. "We must do whatever it takes to secure the fur trade for ourselves. If necessary, we will build more forts at tributaries along the river and at its mouth. We then will be strong enough to exclude both the Dutch and the English from the valley.

"With the Lenape gone and the Hollander and Englishman locked out, we could get four times as many furs and skins from the Susquehannocks.

"What will you do to help us get more beaver furs?" he asked the Lenape sachems before him.

Mattahorn rose to his feet. He stepped forward two steps toward Governor Printz so that he now stood ten feet directly in front of the huge figure seated before him.

"Governor Printz, Great Sachem of the Swedes," he began.

We have come here today to speak of matters of large importance. Thank you for receiving us kindly. While you have received us as guests at your table and in your village, we have come here to remind you that you are OUR guests in OUR homeland.

Governor Printz, perhaps you do not know, and perhaps you do not wish to know, but we treated with Captain Minuit for only a little ground; just enough for him to build a house and grow his crops. That ground was clearly bounded by six trees that to this day carry the mark of the turtle I cut with my own knife and tomahawk. In return, Captain Minuit gave us as presents a kettle, the blankets we wear on our shoulders, and a few other trinkets. He promised us half of the tobacco he grew upon the ground. We have never received any tobacco.

Governor Printz, on the same day we treated with Minuit, we made it as plain to him as the sun in the sky that the Dutch were abusing our red brethren at Drunk Island and that we feared the Dutch would try to drive us likewise from our own homeland. On that day we agreed to let the Swedes dwell among us in OUR homeland, if they would protect us from the Dutch and if they would live peaceably among us. Our word has not changed.

Governor Printz, today the birds of the forest sing sad songs to us. The birds tell us that at Drunk Island, Madman Kieft[61] kills our brethren by the hundreds. He loads some on slave ships never to be seen again. He prays to the same God you pray to and then sends rabid soldiers forth in the middle of the night to the villages of our brethren. They slay in the beds; they tear babes from the mothers' arms and hack them to pieces with their long knives in the very presence of the mothers; boys and girls of tender years they throw into the river, and when the parents try to rescue them, the soldiers drown them all in the icy waters; the fiends cut the hands or feet off some; they open the bellies of still others, and the poor creatures are left to go about holding their bowels in their arms for a short time. And when the soldiers return to Madman Kieft carrying bloody heads to him, he again prays to his God and thanks him. The Dutch wish to kill all the red men and send them to a place they call hell.

Governor Printz, are there only evil manitos among the Schwanneks? Will all Schwanneks indeed kill and

---

[61] The Dutch governor of New Amsterdam who replaced Peter Minuit.

butcher to steal a bit of land they themselves cannot keep? We do not know.

Governor Printz, we do know that good and evil cannot dwell together in one man. So we ask you today: Does good dwell in your hearts or is it evil toward us?

Governor Printz, the downriver Lenape are not a warlike people such as the Mengwe or the Susquehannocks. We want only to live peaceably in our homeland here along the Lenape River. We want no part of your murderous quarrels with other nations across the Great Sea.

Governor Printz, today you have thrown the tomahawk at our feet.

Mattahorn paused, whirled about, and in one lightning movement flung his own tomahawk in front of the sachems. Then he whirled about again and stepped another step closer to Governor Printz.

If you are threatening to drive us from our homeland, I will pick up the tomahawk. All the Lenape will rise as one man and knock you in the head.

Governor Printz, you are yet small in number and help is far away. Your guns are helpless against mosquitoes, and the great guns cannot travel through the woods. Your best houses cannot quench fire, and your strongest soldiers must have food and water.

Governor Printz, if you do not wish to live peaceably among us, we will make your villages and forts as Swanendael. We see that Eesanques was right when he said, "The Schwanneks are different—

English, French, Dutch, and Swede—yet are they all the same. Schwanneks will do anything to own a piece of ground, and the piece is never big enough."

Governor Printz, you are a wise and strong sachem. Do you and your people wish to live peaceably with us in OUR homeland? Will you, according to our agreement with Captain Minuit, help protect us from the Dutch? Will you pick up the tomahawk you have this day flung before us, or shall I pick it up and stick it in your head?

Mattahorn turned quietly, walked discreetly around the tomahawk, and resumed his seat on the floor.

The room lay deathly quiet. Governor Printz sat still, his beady eyes fixed on the ceiling in the back of the room. Pastor Campanius closed his eyes and folded his hands together. Soldiers and officials stared at the tomahawk as if it lay coiled and ready to strike. Five Lenape sachems sat motionless, their eyes watching Governor Printz's giant heaving belly.[62] For a long time Governor Printz brooded in silence.

At last Governor Printz rose unsteadily to his feet. "I beg of you to be excused from the chamber and to have Pastor Campanius in attendance. Please remain here, and we will return to you with an answer."

Time passed. More time passed. Five Lenape sachems sat motionless. The tomahawk steel caught a glint of afternoon sun and reflected it onto the back of the great chair.

The door opened. Pastor Campanius came in first, walked slowly past the great chair, and resumed his seat on the bench. Then came Governor Printz carrying some parchments. He handed them to the secretary and then walked slowly to the great chair. This time he did not sit down. The ray of reflected

---

[62] Governor Printz was reported to weigh 400 lbs. The Indians called him Big Belly.

sunlight from the tomahawk fell on the governor's soiled black robe ... at knee level. His eyes were steady now. His voice held a firm but kinder and gentler tone than before as he began speaking.

Friends, this day I have sinned against God, against Queen Christina, and against you. I know that God is not pleased with what the Dutch are doing at Drunk Island, for His Word tells us "to have mercy and to do justice." Yet even today I have talked of doing the same thing to you as the Dutch are doing at Drunk Island. Pastor Campanius has prayed for me. May God have mercy on me.

Friends, today I have also sinned against Queen Christina and her government. I will explain how this is so. Just a few years ago I was the commander of a great army defending the city of Chemitz. The battle went against us, and I surrendered my army and the city to the Saxon Army. An army court tried me and found that I had done no wrong. Yet the trial was painful, and I feared my career was at an end. But just a little over two years ago I was restored to the Queen's favor. She knighted me and raised me up from my state of disgrace to be governor of New Sweden. She gave me very specific instructions which I must obey. Today, I have grossly disobeyed her orders. I have brought a copy of her orders along, and I now ask the secretary to read certain portions of them to you.

The secretary read from the papers Governor Printz laid on his table.

The wild nations, bordering on all sides,

the governor shall treat with all humanity and
respect, so that no violence or wrong be done
to them by Her Royal Majesty or her subjects
aforesaid; but he shall rather ... exert himself
that the same wild people may be gradually
instructed in the truths and worship of the
Christian religion, and in other ways brought
to civilization and good government, and in
this manner properly guided. Especially shall
he seek to gain their confidence and impress
upon their minds that neither he, the governor,
nor his people and subordinates are come into
these parts to do them any wrong, or injury,
but much more for the purpose of furnishing
them with such things as they may need for the
ordinary wants of life.

Further, the governor must bear in mind
that the wild inhabitants of the country are its
rightful lords.

And, as regards religion, both the Lutheran
Confession and the pretended reformed
religion may be established and observed in
such manner that those who profess the one
or the other religion shall live in peace with
one another, abstaining from all scandal and
abuse. Moreover, ministers and schoolmasters
shall have at heart the conversion of the pagan
inhabitants to Christianity.

Friends, today you see how badly I have disobeyed
the Queen's orders concerning the Lenape. I promise
all who hear me this day that I shall be more faithful
from this day forward.

Friends, today (here Governor Printz placed his
palms together with the fingers pointed upward
and looked pleadingly into the face of each one as
he called his name), Sachem Mattahorn, Sachem
Mitatsemint, Sachem Elupacken, Sachem Mahamen,
and Sachem Chiton, I have also sinned against you. I
have accused you of lying and threatened to kill you.
I ask you to pardon me, and I promise that from this
day forward, as governor of New Sweden, I shall deal
fairly, justly, and kindly with you and your people.

With that solemn promise, Governor Printz walked forward
and bent his hulking frame down on one knee before the
dreadful tomahawk. Clutching the tomahawk in his hand, he
stood to his feet as five Lenape sachems rose with him.

"Friend Mattahorn," he said as he extended the tomahawk
toward the sachem, "I have no need to use this dreadful
weapon against you. Your enemies shall be my enemies and
your friends my friends. I and my people would like to live
among the Lenape in peace in YOUR homeland. Please take
this tomahawk and return it to your bosom."

Mattahorn carefully took the tomahawk and returned it to
its sling on his belt. Then he took the governor's right hand
in his right hand, and the governor's left hand he gripped in
his own. "Friend Printz," he said, "I have heard your words.
You have spoken good words. You now speak from the heart
and not just from the lips. Time will tell if your deeds are
those of the eagle or those of the frog. But if you follow the
kindness and goodness of the Great Spirit, you will know that
the Lenape are your friends. We will live in love with Johan
Printz and his children as long as the creeks and rivers run,
and while the sun, moon, and stars endure."

Mattahorn released his grip on Governor Printz's hands and

stepped back into the semicircle with the other sachems. Each of the five sachems lifted his right hand over his left arm and lightly stroked it three times.

Governor Printz, his officials, the soldiers, the secretary, the interpreters, and Pastor Campanius all did the same thing.

The summer sun was settling toward the horizon when the meeting ended. Warriors and sachems drifted toward the dock.

Berthed at the dock lay the *Kalmar Nyckel.* Mattahorn recognized the ship as the same one the sachems had been on six years earlier when they treated with Peter Minuit. "Could we board the ship?" Mattahorn asked of the escort. With some effort the captain of the ship was located. He was most happy to show his ship to anyone who wished to see it. He hurried to the dock to take the Lenape sachems aboard.

"We have been on board this ship before," Mattahorn stated by way of meeting.

"Really?" asked the captain.

"Yes. Captain Minuit brought us on board when he bought the land where Christina now stands," Mattahorn explained. "We well remember that day."

"Take this tomahawk and return it to your bosom."

—*Governor Johan Printz (Big Belly)*

CQ107

"This has been a good and trusty ship, and she has made many trips across the Great Sea."[63] The captain spoke affectionately of the ship, referring to "she" as though the ship were a woman of intimate friendship.

"Tell me," Mattahorn asked of the captain, "how long does it take to travel across the Great Sea to the Lenape River?"

"We remain on the sea for four moons," the captain replied.

"And how do you guide the ship when the sea always looks the same? I can see how the rudder makes the *Kalmar Nyckel* sail in the direction the captain wants to go. He goes first one direction and then another. Back and forth. The ground swings beneath him. How does the captain know where the ship is? When the sky is dark for many nights and the clouds hide the sun, how does the captain keep from sailing in a great circle?"

"This is a good question. Come. Look at this instrument. We call it a compass. It always points in the direction of Polaris, or the North Star. Do you know of the North Star?"

All five sachems nodded and the captain went on. "It is the star that is always at the same place in the sky. Even in the day the North Star still shines though we cannot see it. When the sky is clouded over at night, the star still shines though we cannot see it. But even though we cannot see the North Star, the finger of this instrument always points in the same direction as that star, to the north."

Mattahorn watched the dancing finger as the captain turned the dial back and forth beneath it. Sure enough, the finger always settled down pointing north. Mattahorn still was not satisfied. "In the forest we may travel for many days to reach where we want to go. We may go north and then south to go around a mountain when we really want to go west. Or

---

[63] The *Kalmar Nyckel* (Key of Calmar) made more successful trips across the ocean than any similar ship of the era.

we may follow a path that takes us to a crossing at a stream. But there are no paths in the sea. If you are always guided by the jumping finger, how do you know how far to the north you are when you are going west? Your eyes see no mountain peaks; your moccasins have no streams to follow. After a journey of four moons, how can you always find the Lenape River?"

With a flourish the captain brought out another box, opened it, and held before his guests a metal disk mounted vertically on a circular frame. "With this instrument we can measure the angle made by the horizon and the North Star. If we know that angle, we can tell how far to the north the ship is. We call this measurement our latitude. Tinicum Island lies at thirty-nine degrees and fifty minutes latitude. We know that the mouth of the Lenape Bay lies at thirty-eight degrees and fifty minutes latitude. So when we have sailed far enough west, we must be at thirty-eight degrees and fifty minutes to find the entrance to the bay."

The captain explained further: "It does not have to be night for us to find our latitude. We can also find how far to the north the ship is by measuring the angle of the sun and the horizon. The instrument we use to do this is called a backstaff."

The captain placed the astrolabe back in the box and picked up a contraption made of four straight sticks attached to one another with two arcs fastened to them at opposing angles. Every sachem listened as the captain went on.

"Fifty years ago an Englishman invented this odd-looking instrument.[64] It is called a backstaff because the one who uses it stands with his back to the sun. With all the older

[64] With this amazing invention the navigator could determine high noon with an accuracy of ± 2 seconds. The instrument does this without any lenses or other high-tech gadgets. An ingenious arrangement of arcs and vanes on the staff allows the observer to use the sun's shadow to give him the exact angle between the sun and the horizon.

instruments, the observer had to peer directly at the high noon sun to take the reading. With the backstaff, one uses the sun's shadow to find the angle made by the sun and the horizon."

The captain held the instrument in front of him and demonstrated how he would take a reading. "The backstaff tells us the angle of the sun and the horizon at high noon," he went on. "We look that angle up on the charts the Portuguese made. Presto. We know exactly how far north the ship sails on the path of the sea.

"Finding the distance we have come west is not so easy."[65] Again the captain paused, strode over to the edge of the cabin, and pointed to two double-domed glasses suspended from the ceiling. "These," said the captain, "are called hourglasses. If you look closely, you will see white sand trickling from the top glass teardrop through the tiny hole into the bottom teardrop. The sand is always flowing. When the top teardrop is empty of sand, the helmsman will always be there to turn it over to let the sand run through the neck again; the helmsman will turn the hourglass over twenty-four times from high noon to high noon."

"Will it always be twenty-four times?" Mattahorn inquired. "Could it sometimes be twenty-three times from high noon to high noon?"

The captain laughed. "Everywhere on earth that I have ever been—on land or on the sea, spring, summer, fall, or winter—it is always twenty-four hours from high noon to high noon, *if you do not move east or west*. Unless the Almighty tinkers with the sun, it will always be that way.

[65] With the astrolabe and the backstaff and established charts, it was possible for the captain to accurately determine the ship's latitude. But it was 1761, 117 years later, before an Englishman, John Harrison, built an accurate seaworthy clock essential for determining a ship's longitude. On a two-month test voyage to Jamaica, his clock lost only eight seconds, and hence Harrison qualified for a £20,000 prize offered by Parliament forty-seven years earlier in 1714.

"But if you sail east, it will be less than twenty-four hours from high noon to high noon. If you sail west, it will be more than twenty-four hours from high noon to high noon.

"Because this time difference in a day gives us a very rough idea of how far east or west we have come, we track it very closely. We even use a second half-hour glass that the helmsman turns over twice each hour. That way the two glasses keep check on each other. Even the best hourglasses mess up at times."

The captain laughed again. "No matter how careful we are with our measurements and our timekeeping, every ship captain I know has been lost sometime or other. But not a one of them will own up to it."

"Why don't the birds get lost?" Mattahorn inquired. "Why don't the fish get lost?"

"The fish and the birds keep us humble," the captain replied. "We don't know how they navigate. All I know is that the hourglass, astrolabe, backstaff, and compass are wonderful inventions to aid the captain. But they aren't perfect. Sometimes the sea can be an awesome beast to ride. I have sailed when we could not see the sun by day nor the stars by night for many days. The backstaff and the astrolabe were both useless. At other times the sea was too violent to take a reading. Then we sailed onward by 'dead reckoning.'

"Dead reckoning is judgment. That's what 'tis." The captain drew himself up especially tall and straight before continuing. " 'Tis the storms that separate the real captains from the skippers, and I don't mean how many storms he can sail through. Any fool can start out with these inventions, but unless a skipper has judgment, he'll sail straight into every storm he can find. The real captain avoids as many storms as possible. That takes judgment."

When Mattahorn stepped off the *Kalmar Nyckel,* a young Swedish boy about ten years of age timidly approached. "May I speak with the Great Sachem Mattahorn?" the lad asked in fluent Lenape.

Mattahorn liked the boy at once, for the lad showed not only a native grasp of the Lenape tongue, but also the proper native respect for an elder. Mattahorn stepped aside and asked, "What is the message that you bear?"

"Pastor Campanius invites you to spend the night at his house," the boy announced. "He is ready to receive you now."

"Should I bring others with me?" Mattahorn asked.

"The pastor's house is small, and the nature of the matters he wishes to discuss are large. Pastor Campanius would be glad if you could journey by yourself," the lad responded.

"Very well, then. If you will wait for me until the others have departed, I will go with you."

Mattahorn gathered the other four sachems together and informed them of his plans to stay on Tinicum Island a while longer. They talked briefly of the coming council fire of the Lenape to be held over the full moon of roasting ears at Shackamoxon.[66] He confirmed with them that the messengers had already been sent out.

Mattahorn sent word of his continued stay at Tinicum Island with those from his village. Then he, the Great Sachem of the Lenape, turned and followed a mere boy into the growing darkness. In the years to come, the destiny of the Lenape would swing heavily on the shoulders of those two.

Mattahorn and the lad trudged silently along single file till they

---

[66] Present Kensington in Philadelphia. Shackamoxon was the traditional meeting place of the Lenape nation. The head chief of the Turtle Clan presided over council fires held at this place.

reached Pastor Campanius's new log home. The pastor seated the lad and the sachem next to a smoking low fire outside the one-room cabin, then offered them more of the *sappan* and other meats and berries left from earlier in the day.

After all three of them were again satisfied and had eaten their fill, they relaxed around the low fire.

"Lad," Mattahorn asked, "what name do you bear?"

"My father's name is Peter Larsson Cock,[67] and he has given me the name Lars Cock.[68] Others call me Lasse or Laussa," the boy answered.

"His father was one of the officials who sat beside me at the council today," added Pastor Campanius. "Besides that, Lasse is my Lenape teacher, and a good one at that."

"Tell me," mused Mattahorn, "what is time? The captain on the *Kalmar Nyckel* spoke to us of dividing the day into twenty-four equal parts. He showed us an instrument called an hourglass. Do you understand what time is? The interpreter on the ship could not think of any Lenape word for it. Lasse, do you know of any Lenape word for time?"

"No, Sachem, I do not know of a Lenape word for time, but I will explain the meaning to you," said the boy. Here he jumped up from his log seat, picked up a stick, and drew two circles in the dirt directly beside Mattahorn. Then he carefully divided each circle into twelve parts. "This picture is not as round nor as exact as you would make it," said the

---

[67] Peter Larsson came over on the ship Charitas in 1641. He served as cook or "Kock" on the ship and hence the English name Cock. His descendants later changed the name to Cox. In 1643, thirty-three-year-old Peter married seventeen-year-old Margaret Svensson, who bore him thirteen children. Peter served as a justice in the courts under Swedish, Dutch, and English administrations until he retired in 1680.

[68] Lars (Lasse) Cock was the oldest son of Peter Cock. He was born in New Sweden on March 21, 1646, twelve years later than portrayed. Historical records tell us Lasse became a trader, a translator for William Penn, a justice, a member of the Provincial Council, and numerous times a member of the Colonial Assembly. He married Martha Ashman on May 15, 1669. She was born of English parents at Long Island, New York, in August of 1650. They were the parents of thirteen children. He died at Passayunk in October of 1699.

lad modestly. "But we shall imagine that the one circle is the moon and the other circle is the sun. The moon represents the night and the sun represents the day. If I could draw better, each part of the sun and the moon would be exactly equal, and each part would represent one hour. So the day has twelve hours and the night has twelve hours. Any part of the day or night that has passed we call time." Lasse resumed his seat on the log, confident that he had fairly represented the concept to Mattahorn.

"Well done, lad," exclaimed Mattahorn. "Then time is an hour. Like an hourglass. Then time is twelve hours, for you have shown me there are twelve parts in the day and twelve parts in the night. But why are there twelve parts in the day and twelve parts in the night? Why are there not seven parts or ten parts in the day and the night?"

Lasse glanced helplessly at Pastor Campanius. Pastor Campanius had a puzzled look on his face. Lasse translated the discussion and the question for Pastor Campanius. Then Lasse said to Mattahorn, "I do not know, Sachem, why there are twelve hours in the day and twelve hours in the night."

"Lad," Mattahorn continued, "I see that you are an honest fellow and that you are wise beyond your years. There are many things that the oldest and wisest among us do not know. But it is the greatest of wisdom to tell the truth.

"The truth is that you do not know why there are twelve hours in the day or the night. Neither do I know why the turtle has twelve parts painted on its shell. But if the Great Spirit chose to paint twelve segments on the turtle's house, why should I not learn from what he would teach me?

"Perhaps the white man's God divided the day and the night into twelve parts as well, although I have never seen twelve parts painted on the day or the night.

"And did you not say that the day and night are equal in length? How can this be? Here along the Lenape River we do not make the day or the night. The Great Spirit makes the day and the night. In winter the day is shorter than the night. In summer the night is shorter than the day. Day and night are not equal.

"Why should we try to make day and night equal when they are not? The sun will rise when it is ready. The moon will come when it is ready. Things take as long as they take. We cannot change them by dividing the day and night into parts. It is better to dance to the rhythm of the earth and the sky than it is to follow a beat from a man-made drum. For the song of the earth and the sky rests the spirit, whereas a man-made beat brings only weariness to his bones.

"Then what is time? Time appears to me as nothing more than the beat from a white man's drum. It deafens him with its beat and silences the music of the earth and sky around him.

"Listen. Be still. Wait. Can you not hear the song of the earth and the sky?"

The three listened. The summer full moon climbed to its highest point, then started falling toward the west. The hoots of the owls, the calling of the whippoorwills, the croaking of the frogs, and the continual chirping of the katydids made plenty of noise. A mockingbird went through his whole repertoire several times. One could not say it was quiet.

Perhaps eyelids closed and shoulders drooped, but all three listened, the elder sachem, the seasoned pastor, and the innocent lad. Around them they heard the sounds of the summer night infused with the music of life. They felt the rhythm of the earth and the sky. They felt the throb of centuries pulsing through the present. Their spirits rested in a world where time did not matter.

Only a few coals still glowed when Mattahorn broke the trance. He arose briefly and added two small sticks to the fire. Mattahorn sat on the ground once more and addressed Pastor Campanius.

"Pastor Campanius," Mattahorn began, "you do well with the Lenape for being in the country only a little over a year. But I am glad your teacher continues with us, for I wish to speak with you of matters besides diet and custom, and I wish to be sure that we understand each other."

"Yes, we need Lasse and his ready tongue," Pastor Campanius agreed. "I, too, must be clearly understood, for I speak for another and not for myself."

"Pastor Green Leaf,[69] if I may call you such, why does a man your age come to New Sweden?"

"Yes, Sachem Mattahorn, I have come to New Sweden to advise the settlers about things of God and things of the Spirit. I am to be the preacher for the settlement, and it is also my duty to teach the natives the things of God. To do that I must learn the Lenape tongue and put it into writing so that the writings of our great teachers may be taught to the Lenape."

"Pastor Green Leaf, I do not understand. The Lenape would think that before a man can teach he must first learn from the elder. How can an eaglet tell what he has seen from the heights before he soars above the mountains? And even when the eaglet has seen, he does not gain wisdom or understanding. Those things come slowly with age and experience. The Lenape believe that even the spirits of the rocks can teach us many things because they are some of the

---

[69] Johan Campanius Holm (1601-1683) came to America in 1643 at age forty-two. He translated Luther's Catechism and several Bible passages into Lenape and was well respected by the Lenape Indians. He returned to Sweden "with his many children" at the close of the war in Europe in 1648. His grandson, Thomas Campanius Holm (d. 1702), published some of the earliest descriptions of New Sweden based on his grandfather's manuscripts.

oldest spirits around us. How can you advise those older and wiser than yourself?"

"Ah, Sachem Mattahorn, again you speak with wisdom. You are right. The training I received in the school of theology is little compared with wisdom learned in the school of life. But if God calls me to labor for Him, He also will help me. Whereas you have learned the laws of the forest and of men, I have studied the laws of God. I would teach His laws to men.

"Sachem Mattahorn, there is also another concern that brought me to New Sweden. For the past twenty-six years most of the peoples of Europe have been fighting to determine which ruler is really God's king on earth. Three groups strive for the mastery—Catholic, Lutheran, and Reformed. Each group, or so-called church, believes it speaks for God, and that all those on the other side are going to hell. Soldiers from every country have been forced into battle on all sides. Great guns destroy forts; armies plunder and burn large cities; thousands and thousands die until there are few men left to till the fields.

"Still the wars go on. Sweden's armies fight on. Queen Christina's own father, the King who dreamed of starting New Sweden, fought in Germany. His army won the battle, but the King lost his life. Year after year the fighting continues. Nothing is accomplished save death and destruction.

"Governor Johan Printz, like myself, as a young man received training in the things of God at a famous German school. Despite his training, he was forced onto the battlefield for eighteen long years. He has seen the horrors and senselessness of war. He hates it. He has determined that I should avoid a fate similar to his and not waste my life in the bloody, senseless wars in Europe. He brought me to New Sweden to save me from such a fate."

"Pastor Green Leaf, it is still not clear to me why the nations of Europe have been fighting for the past twenty-six years."

"Sachem Mattahorn, I know only what I have seen and heard. Is there a reason for the wars? Or are there many reasons? Or is there no reason at all?

"I suspect there are many reasons for the wars, but none of them make any sense. When hatred and anger consume the soul, the mind stops. Would anyone in his right mind willingly sell his life on a battlefield for a few pieces of silver? Will anyone really reap God's blessing for sending infidels to hell? Why do individual soldiers kill and burn and rape and steal? Why do soldiers do things as part of an army that they would never do at home? Is war only a blood sport?

"These are questions good soldiers dare not think about. Good soldiers are only supposed to obey orders, even if they rampage their way straight into hell.

"Sachem Mattahorn, these thoughts torment me. I do not know why men fight in Europe. Yet it does seem to me that my native country, Sweden, has the nobler cause."

Pastor Green Leaf stared into the smoldering fire as he spoke. He wished the smoke could drive the little tormenters from his mind, but if it failed at that, at least it helped keep the mosquitoes away.

Mattahorn sat still, looking straight ahead. Only the occasional puffs of smoke from his pipe revealed his attentiveness to the discussion.

"Pastor Green Leaf, neither do I know why Schwanneks kill and steal in Europe. But I do know why the Schwanneks kill and steal at Drunk Island. The Schwanneks want furs and they want land.

"Pastor Green Leaf, are the Swedes here the same as the Dutch at Drunk Island? Are they all Schwanneks?

"Pastor Green Leaf, tell me more about Governor Big Belly. Men are not born with strength or wisdom. And a warrior as strong as he has been tested before."

"Ah, Sachem Mattahorn, 'tis true," responded Pastor Green Leaf. "Both the foolish and the wise begin life as babes. And yet some become wise and some become foolish. Is it the blood that courses through the veins that makes the difference? Or do some stumble upon truth while others never find truth in the path they travel? Or does God alone choose who will become wise and who will become foolish?

"Sachem Mattahorn, as you have noted, Governor Big Belly is a strong man. He has been tested many years in battle. But battle can tempt a man to think that might makes right, that because he can conquer he is right. Perhaps, at times, Governor Printz has yielded to that temptation. It seems easy for him to think that bullets and cannonballs can solve every problem.

"Sachem Mattahorn, Governor Big Belly is a just and fair man. He may think that justice belongs to the victor, and it may be true, for a weak man cannot extract justice from a strong man.

"Sachem Mattahorn, Governor Big Belly also fears God and the Queen. He knows that he will be held accountable to both God and Queen Christina for what he does as governor. Today he gave his enemies a large tomahawk to sink into his head if he disobeys the Queen's orders that were read at the council. His orders are 'to bear in mind that the wild inhabitants of the country are its rightful lords.' He was commanded to treat all natives 'with all humanity and respect so that no violence or wrong be done to them.' Any grievance or injustice against the natives need only be reported to Sweden. If found true, Governor Big Belly will at once be as a mighty oak struck by lightning. Big Belly knows that.

"Sachem Mattahorn, I do not believe New Sweden will be like New Netherland. The Swedes are different from the Dutch. The lands along the Lenape River will not be like the killing grounds of Drunk Island. The governor of New Sweden is commanded to treat all natives fairly and to recognize you as the rightful owners of the land. That is not true of the Dutch at Drunk Island.

"There is another important difference that you heard at the council but may not have understood. In New Sweden, believers of both the Lutheran Confession and the Reformed Confession are to be allowed to live together as long as they live here peaceably. This is different than it is in all of Europe. This is different than it is at Drunk Island. At Drunk Island and in Europe everyone must be a member of one religion—Catholic, Lutheran, Reformed—or else be enslaved, homes and goods stolen, jailed, killed, or exiled. Sometimes one may be Lutheran for a year or two and then he must be Catholic for a while. So besides allowing the natives to live in peace, in New Sweden we are even going to allow people of another religion to live among us.

"Can people of different nations and religions live together in peace? It has not worked for hundreds of years in Europe. Will it work in New Sweden? We will see."

Again, Mattahorn reflected for some time before speaking. "Pastor Green Leaf, you seem to think that Governor Printz can be trusted to keep the promises he made today." Mattahorn paused before continuing. "Once when hunting I wounded a great black bear. The bear, when he saw the fight was useless, cried and whimpered piteously. So the questions I must measure are these: Are the governor's whimpers only those of the wounded bear? If he is allowed to return to the forest, will he again become a powerful and dangerous foe? Those two questions cannot be cooked in a small kettle. Instead, we will cook them in a large kettle at a great council of the Lenape two moons from tonight at Shackamoxon."

Mattahorn blew four rings of smoke from his pipe, each one ascending in the exact path of the one before it. He then handed the pipe to Green Leaf, who likewise took four quick puffs. The smoke went every which way, but Mattahorn seemed not to notice. He took the pipe and tapped it carefully against a stone next to his feet. As he rose to his feet, the first light of dawn was breaking the eastern sky. Mattahorn faced that light standing tall and erect, lifted his right arm upward with the index and middle finger extended, and began to chant:

> *Great Spirit,*
> *Maker of the sky, the earth, the sun, the moon,*
> *Keeper of the spirits of the fish, the birds, the animals, the*
> *trees, the stones,*
> *Guardian of the Four Winds,*
> *Thank you for bringing light again to the People of the*
> *Dawn.*
> *Thank you for sending fire to warm our houses and cook our*
> *food.*
> *Thank you for bringing water to inspire the ground and to*
> *quench our thirst.*
> *Thank you for the ground to grow the maize and the deer to*
> *give us meat.*
> *For the ancient song of the Lenape,*
> *For the everlasting sun that rises this day,*
> *I, Mattahorn, the Great Sachem of the Lenni Lenape,*
> *thank you.*

When Mattahorn had finished his chant, he took a small pinch of tobacco from his pouch with his left hand and sprinkled it on the ground before him. Then he stood motionless with his right arm still raised and his two fingers pointed upward.

At last Mattahorn turned to say farewell and begin his journey home. Pastor Green Leaf stopped him.

"Sachem Mattahorn, there is yet one matter I am forced to mention. Governor Printz must have more furs and skins. The cost of maintaining the settlement grows every day." Pastor Campanius winked at Mattahorn. "Governor Printz must feed the settlers and the soldiers if he is going to protect the Lenape from the Dutch. What can you do to help him gain more furs and skins?"

"Pastor Green Leaf, that is another question we must cook in the large kettle at Shackamoxon.[70] Meanwhile, you can tell Governor Big Belly that his words have not fallen to the ground."

Again Mattahorn turned to go and Lasse fell in step beside him. Lasse reached up and took hold of Mattahorn's hand. "Sachem Mattahorn," he said in his boyish voice, "I would like to ask a question of the Great Sachem."

Mattahorn turned and looked down at Lasse. Then he reached out and took the lad's other hand also into his own. "My lad, what would you like to ask?" he said tenderly.

"Great Sachem, did you not say that there are twelve divisions on the turtle's carapace? I think I have counted thirteen on the turtle. And are there not thirteen spots on the turtle on your breast?"

Mattahorn waited a long time before answering. "Lasse, you have touched one of the great mysteries of the Lenape. We

---

[70] Mattahorn did preside over a great council fire at Shackamoxon where the annihilation of the Swedes was considered.

seldom speak of this, but I will try to explain. There are twelve manitos in the spirit world. The Great Spirit sits atop them all. The Great Spirit's spot is sacred to the Lenape because out of the Great Spirit's spot on the turtle's shell came the earth. The Lenape do not count that spot. So the turtle has only twelve divisions. Do you understand?"

"Thank you, Great Sachem," Lasse whispered reverently.

Mattahorn turned and walked quietly toward the waiting canoe. Lasse trailed him. Carefully he placed each of his small feet lightly in the sachem's footsteps.

Before the Lenape council convened at Shackamoxon, another event occurred that shook the uneasy truce between the Swedes and the Lenape. Some young braves killed a Swedish woman and her husband, an Englishman, in one of the outlying cabins close to Chester. The same braves burned a sawmill and the lumber already cut to build a ship.

Governor Big Belly responded swiftly. He moved cannon and soldiers into a defensive position around the town[71] directly west of Tinicum Island. But the message was plain: "One more problem, and we will kill also."

Mattahorn again gathered up the four chiefs and again made his way to Printz Hall. After the proper greetings and ceremonies had been performed, Mattahorn came to the point of the visit.

"Governor Printz, we have looked into the matter of the murder and the burning. The Indians who murdered and burned had a private quarrel over the site of the cabin and the matter of cutting trees for the sawmill. The Lenape custom

---

[71] Settlement of Chester, Pennsylvania.

is that the blood relatives of the slain punish those who have committed the murders and the burnings. Or the murderers may try to appease the relatives with satisfactory gifts. Offenders also may try to restore goods burned or stolen and thus satisfy the blood relatives.

"Governor Printz, this burning and murder was not an act of war. It was the result of white people encroaching on Lenape lands and using them without the consent of the Lenape. Many more such acts will come if your people do not remember that you are our guests and must dwell here on good terms with the Lenape. We as sachems cannot prevent private quarrels from flaring into violence, but we do not want it."

Governor Big Belly cleared his throat as though he would speak, but Mattahorn continued. "Governor Printz, it is not our custom that a speaker should be interrupted. When I am finished, then you shall have your time, and we will listen with patience."

Governor Printz reddened at the rebuke. He was not used to deferring to "ignorant savages," and it plainly angered him to be taught proper manners by uncivilized heathen.

"Governor Printz, what shall the Lenape do when settlers take the land from them and attempt to drive them away from their own homes? What shall we sachems do when Swedes drive our people out of our homeland? What shall we sachems do when Swedes destroy the trees on land they have never purchased from the Lenape? We sachems want peace with the Swedes, and we will do our best to prevent future attacks on Swedish settlers. Yet we cannot restrain settlers who so boldly settle on our lands without respect for Lenape claims. You Swedes must remember that the Lenape were here first. It is OUR homeland.

"Governor Printz, the Lenape do want the Swedes in our homeland to trade with us and to protect us from the Dutch. The Dutch do not trade fairly. The Dutch drive out our brethren, the Mohicans, from their homes at Drunk Island and along the Mohican River. The Dutch arm the Mengwe and use them to kill the Mohicans, the Susquehannocks, and the Lenape as well. So we, the Lenape, do want the Swedes here to trade with us and to help us. The Lenape and our allies, the Susquehannocks, do want peace with the Swedes.

"Governor Printz, will you give us this peace? May our friends be your friends and our enemies your enemies?"

Governor Printz had by now regained his normal color ... and his normal bravado.

"Sachem Mattahorn," he began, "I too want peace with the Lenape and the Susquehannocks. The Swedes want to trade with the Lenape and the Susquehannocks.

"Sachem Mattahorn, I have told you before that we have justly bought the lands in this river valley. We will not pay for them a second time. You claim rights to this valley because you were here first. So what!" Printz roared. "The devil is also the oldest proprietor in hell, but even he might give place to a younger one.

"Sachem Mattahorn," Printz continued in a more normal tone, "it is doubtful that you sachems had nothing to do with the murders and the burning. If you would stop griping about the land ownership and accept the advance of the Christian nations among you, fewer of these so-called private quarrels would develop. There could be peace.

"Sachem Mattahorn, you have lectured me about the customs of the Lenape. You say that it is up to the blood relatives to avenge the death of kin. After someone is killed, it is too late. It is much better if the dispute can be settled before someone is killed. Let me tell you what our custom is where there is a dispute. If two parties have a quarrel, they bring it to me. Each side tells me its complaint and presents all the evidence it can to support its claims. Both sides may bring others also to speak in their favor. Each witness swears by God's Holy Book to tell the truth. When each side is finished, I must think about the code that has been written on the subject. Then I determine which side is telling the truth and render a decision based on the code. If the two quarreling parties do not like my decision, the soldiers see to it that my decision is carried out. Does that not sound to you like a peaceful way to avoid bloodshed?

"Sachem Mattahorn, we will make peace again. This once I will overlook the blood that has been shed and the burning of the lumber. I will hold you sachems personally responsible to keep the peace. And I assure you that if there is any more trouble, I will not let a soul of you savages live."

Governor Printz's beady snake eyes focused carefully on Mattahorn. Like a snake ready to strike, he locked his eyes on his prey.

Mattahorn rose to his feet and leaned very close upon the governor. "Very well," replied Mattahorn without a flicker of emotion. "I suppose you have made a fair bargain. So I will make an equal one with you. The Lenape will renew our peace with the Swedes. But if one of your soldiers or one of the Swedish settlers makes any trouble with the Lenape, we shall kill every Swede that lives along the Lenape River. We shall kill young and old from the babe to the governor. The Swedes shall be as the Dutch at Swanendael.

"Governor Printz, is that the kind of peace pact you wish to make? Do you want a peace based on the fear that we must kill or be killed? Or would you like a peace pact of a gentler nature, by which Swede and Lenape can dwell side by side, trading together freely, and united against our common foe, the Dutch?

"Is that the peace you want here in the Lenape homeland? As Ever-Be-Joyful said, 'Cold blood only brings forth hot blood.' Can peace spring forth from murder?

"Pastor Campanius teaches that Christians ought to love one another. Then he tells me Christians have been killing one another for thirty years on the battlefields of Europe. Madman Kieft wishes to kill all the Mohicans and any Lenape he can find. If he succeeds in killing all the Indians, plundering their goods, and taking all their lands, will that bring peace? No. It will not. For before the blood runs cold, he will be attacking the Swedes on the Lenape River, and ere that blood be shed, a stronger will plunder him. Cold blood begets hot blood and evil begets death."

Narrated by Glikkikan

"So what kind of man was Big Belly?" I asked Owechela. "Was he just and fair or mean and cruel? Was he good or evil?"

"Glikkikan," Owechela began, "to answer your questions I will need to tell you some more about Big Belly.

"Mattahorn had good reasons why he never trusted Big Belly. Pastor Green Leaf told Mattahorn how Big Belly had described the Lenape in a letter to one of his friends:

> They are big and strong, well-built men; paint themselves terribly in the face, differently, not one like unto the other, and go about with only a piece

of cloth about half an ell broad around the waist
and down about the hips. They are revengeful,
cunning in dealings and doing, clever in making all
kinds of things from lead, copper, and tin, and also
carve skillfully in wood. They are good and quick
marksmen with their arrows and, above all, *are not to
be trusted.*

"So you see, Big Belly did not trust the Lenape and always
tried to deal with them as his servants.

"Pastor Green Leaf was not that way. Green Leaf's five years
of teaching and preaching among the Lenape helped maintain
a tenuous peace between the Swedes and the Lenape. Then
the war in Europe ended and Green Leaf hurried home.

"Without Green Leaf around to temper his fits, Big Belly
proved an aggressive foe to anything or anyone he viewed as in
his way. That even included his own countrymen.

"When Big Belly encountered dissatisfaction among the
Swedes, he himself tried the leader of the opposition, Anders
Jonsson, and had him executed."

When Owechela told me this story, I still remember how
his lips pinched tightly together and he spit out, "So much for
Schwannek justice."

Then Owechela rushed on, saying, "Another settler, Clemet
the Finn, claimed ownership of a flour mill. Big Belly caught
him inside the church before the meeting ... seized him ...
followed him with blows and strikes ... knocked him to the
ground ... punched him on the ground ... threw him into
the church ... locked him in jail for eight days ... let him do
work for several weeks." And then in a lighter tone, Owechela
mocked, "So much for 'Christian' love."

"Glikkikan, who can tell what is in a man's spirit except by
the deeds he does? Many of Big Belly's deeds were evil. He was

always selfish. He refused to live at peace with anyone, even other Schwanneks. The Lenape felt good when Big Belly went home.

"But one good thing Big Belly did do while he lived among the Lenape was to restrain the Dutch from becoming our masters. Mattahorn used Big Belly to hold back the Dutch and English tides in our homeland. If it had not been for Mattahorn ..."

Owechela couldn't say enough good about Mattahorn.

"Yes, Glikkikan," Owechela sang, and his voice was as beautiful as the song of the wood thrush, "Mattahorn was a great chief. But the deeds of his latter days surpass those of the former.

"Listen closely, Glikkikan, and I shall teach you the story of Mattahorn's last days. These are days that I well remember, days when I was but a lad as you are now."

Mattahorn and Morning Light

As told by Owechela

Toward the end of the fawn month, after I had passed ten winters, the Lenape were drawn down to the Lenape River. For ten days eleven ships flying the red, white, and blue flag of the Dutch sailed up and down the river. Four of the larger ships fired their great guns repeatedly. Hundreds of armed men rode on the ships while drummers and flutes made their music. One smaller ship flying the Swedish flag with its blue background and yellow crossbars trailed the larger fleet at a safe distance. The larger fleet carried Strutting Turkey, the governor of Drunk Island.[72] The smaller ship sported Big Belly and twenty-nine Swedes.

I'll never forget those beautiful sailing ships, the booming of the cannons, the beating of the drums, and the whistling of the flutes. It made my body tingle with excitement and stirred

[72] The Dutch governor of New Amsterdam, Peter Stuyvesant.

my blood. *Oh*, I thought, *it would be so much fun to climb one of those tall masts to the basket where the wind ripples the sails and just ride along!*

But these ships were not sailing up and down the Lenape River for sport. These ships sailed the river as part of a mortal struggle between the Dutch and the Swedes over who would own the fur trade ... and the Lenape homeland.

This was not the first time Strutting Turkey tried to push the Swedes aside. Just three years earlier, Strutting Turkey's deputies had paid Mattahorn, Sinques, and Alibakinne to confirm an earlier Dutch purchase for land at Armenveruis.[73] Dutch settlers soon followed to build houses and establish trading points. Big Belly tore down their houses and destroyed any trading points the Dutch tried to establish.

Just two months before the fleet and the soldiers had arrived, in the early part of the planting month, Strutting Turkey had sent a lone armed ship to patrol the Lenape River. Big Belly had immediately confronted the ship with his armed boat, and the lone ship had sailed away.

This time Strutting Turkey was for real. Big Belly dared do nothing against all the armed ships and the hundreds of soldiers. However, Strutting Turkey knew he could not profit from the fur trade or put settlers and traders along the Lenape River unless he secured the goodwill of the Lenape. All the drumming and cannonading he could do would be useless when the ships sailed back to Drunk Island if he left the Lenape like a nest of hornets when somebody is banging on their nest.

Accordingly, Strutting Turkey arranged several conferences with the Lenape, freely giving out gifts and making many promises. The Lenape willingly took his gifts and put their

---

[73] A spot near the mouth of the Schuylkill River, Philadelphia, Pennsylvania.

totem marks on the Dutch land papers.

Mattahorn was not among them. Strutting Turkey was not ignorant. He knew that if the Dutch were going to take control of the South River, as he called the Lenape River, Mattahorn and the other principal sachems of the Lenape must give their consent. The Dutch governor sent word to Sachem Mattahorn, Sachem Pemenetta, and Sachem Sinques,[74] inviting them to meet with him at Fort Nassau.[75] Mattahorn, speaking for all three sachems, declined the invitation.

Disappointed, but not thwarted in his designs, Strutting Turkey sailed his fleet to an unsettled spot, known as the Sand Hook, south of where the Christina enters the Lenape River. There he unloaded two hundred soldiers and settlers, who began the construction of a large fort.

Leaving a portion of his fleet to guard and assist the builders, Strutting Turkey once more sailed north up the Lenape River until he came back to his starting point at Fort Nassau. There the fleet waited while the crews and soldiers loaded the cannons and supplies from the fort onto the ships.

Sachem Mattahorn studied the activities of the Dutch governor and his fleet. He listened closely to the scouts' reports. He conferred with Sachem Pemenetta and Sachem Sinques, but he himself moved from place to place along the Lenape River so that he could observe the fleet and still keep his own whereabouts unknown to the Dutch.

When Mattahorn's scouts reported that the Dutch were preparing to abandon Fort Nassau, he dispatched a lone messenger to the Dutch governor. The message of

[74] The other two of the five sachems had died by this date.

[75] The oldest Dutch fort on the Delaware River erected in 1626 between Newton Creek and Big Timber Creek and now covered by the present city of Gloucester, New Jersey.

the wampum belt Mattahorn sent was this: "If Governor
Stuyvesant cared to treat with Sachem Mattahorn, Sachem
Pemenetta, and Sachem Sinques, he should sail north with
only one ship to the spot where Neshaminy Creek enters the
Lenape River as soon as possible. Upon arriving at Neshaminy
Creek, the governor shall remain on the ship and await
further instructions. If the governor wishes to accept the
invitation to the council fire, he shall return three gifts by the
hand of the messenger."

The messenger returned to Mattahorn carrying three of the
finest knives Mattahorn had ever seen. He rubbed his thumb
carefully along the strong thin edge and nodded approvingly.

At evening the following day, Mattahorn dispatched another
messenger to the mouth of Neshaminy Creek. Sure enough,
a large Dutch ship rested at midstream of the Lenape River.
The messenger approached the large ship cautiously in the
gathering dusk. When he made known that he had another
message for Strutting Turkey, he was quickly lifted on deck
and soon faced the governor.

The message bearer first presented one of the knives the
governor had given to Mattahorn the day before. Stuyvesant
looked briefly at the knife, nodded, and then looked
expectantly at the messenger. "Sachem Mattahorn welcomes
you to the homeland of the Lenape," the messenger began.
"We have begun preparations to treat with you at our Lenape
council fire. When all is in readiness, we will return to the
ship and take you to the council fire. There will be room
for only two people to accompany you—one officer and an
interpreter. When you come to the council fire, you must be
prepared to tell us the present latitude of your ship. Rest well.
The journey will be a tiring one." The message bearer stopped
and with a light movement of one hand indicated the end of

his message.

Strutting Turkey chafed his hands and stomped his wooden leg. He muttered to himself and then fumed to the interpreter, "Tell him that I will not leave the ship without soldiers to escort me. Tell him that he will have to stay on the ship until they come to take me to the council. No, tell him that he will have to remain as a hostage while I am gone."

The messenger showed no visible sign of concern at the governor's anger. He shrugged his shoulders and quietly waited to see what would happen next. Strutting Turkey finally sent the messenger below deck with two burly soldiers to accompany him. "Treat him well, but see that the slippery eel does not slide through our fingers," he ordered.

The night passed quietly and so did the next day. No more messengers appeared nor did any boats come to take Strutting Turkey to the council fire. The prisoner sat motionless, offering no protest while appearing to enjoy the company of his guards. He watched their movements with interest.

At dusk the next evening Strutting Turkey appeared again with his interpreter. "Have they treated you well?" he asked, pointing to the guards. Again, the messenger only shrugged. The commander tried again in a kindly way. "I have a message for Mattahorn. Will you take it to him?"

The messenger slowly rose to his feet and held out his hand. "Where is the wampum?" he asked. "I must have wampum and gifts or the Sachem will not accept the message."

"Of course. Of course. I should have known," Strutting Turkey chided himself impatiently. Then he gave a command to one of the soldiers. The soldier slipped quietly away while Strutting Turkey stomped restlessly back and forth, noisily banging his peg leg along on the floor. The soldier returned carrying a beautiful new gun and some powder. With a slight bow, Strutting Turkey laid the gun in the outstretched hand and hung the powder bag around the messenger's neck.

"Now," he continued, "tell Sachem Mattahorn that I am ready to come to the Lenape council fire. I accept his terms."

"Tell Sachem Mattahorn that Governor Stuyvesant is ready to come to the council fire. Governor Stuyvesant accepts his terms," the messenger repeated.

Strutting Turkey bowed again, and with a wave of his hand bade the messenger to leave.

The messenger returned to Mattahorn at an encampment along Neshaminy Creek. Another night and most of the following day passed. Sachem Pemenetta, Sachem Sinques, and a third special guest, Lasse Cock, arrived at the encampment.

"Lasse," Mattahorn told him, "from now on I shall call you Falling Leaf. You shall be to the Schwanneks as a falling leaf in the forest. The Schwanneks will not see you, but you will see and hear everything. You will be to me as a son, and you will be my eyes and ears as my own grow dim with years."

Mattahorn called the assembled warriors and sachems to gather around the council fire. "All is now ready for us to fetch our guests whom we have invited to the council. I believe it is now safe for us to fetch them. We have separated Strutting Turkey from his main forces, and the proud commander has humbled himself enough to meet our demands. We have ruffled the feathers of Strutting Turkey a bit, but he will be as harmless as a young poult while he is with us, for he needs us very badly. See to it that no ill befalls him while he is under our care. Take three canoes and return under the cover of darkness. We will keep the council fire burning until you return."

Three long dugout canoes holding five warriors, each with one empty space, eased out from the bank into Neshaminy Creek at dusk. It was on toward midnight before the three canoes returned, each bearing one dripping passenger.

The Great Sachem of the Dutch looked like a strutting turkey in the rain. His green velvet knee pants clung to his legs. The red bows adorning each shoe folded limply downward. His white hose sagged around his legs, held in place only by the cord tied tightly below each knee. His wrinkled white shirt with its split sleeves would have fit a man twice as large, and Strutting Turkey was not a small man. His skullcap fit his head like the cap on an acorn. Long hair from his wig dragged his shoulders, the curls dissipated by the rain. The only redeeming glory of the whole man was the silver bands wrapped tightly around his wooden leg.

Mattahorn, Sinques, and Pemenetta, sat around the low fire cross-legged on the forest soil. The sachems wore loincloths with their straight gray hair dangling back to their shoulders. A red blanket draped carefully over the left shoulder of each sachem with a black neck scarf held firmly in place by a golden clasp. A wide silver bracelet hung on each sachem's right arm. The tattooed tortoise stood out boldly, crawling upward across Mattahorn's chest.

The sachems did not rise as their three guests approached the fire. Mattahorn pointed to the logs on the opposite side of the fire and motioned for them to be seated. The sachems and Lasse Cock continued sitting motionless before the fire. The three Dutchmen fidgeted back and forth, staring first at the fire, then into the surrounding forest, and then trying to study their hosts without looking at them. At last the guests, too, sat motionless and relaxed, waiting and listening to the peace of the forest night.

When all was still except for the babbling of Neshaminy Creek, Mattahorn placed two more sticks on the glowing coals of the fire, then reached over and picked up the calumet. Slowly he placed tobacco in the bowl and carefully lit it with a burning twig from the fire. Mattahorn took several draws from the mouthpiece on the long feathered stem and ceremoniously passed it to Sinques. Sinques likewise drew several times on the pipe, then slowly handed it to Pemenetta. After Pemenetta took his turn, he passed the pipe back to Mattahorn, who slowly offered it to Stuyvesant. Stuyvesant made a few expert puffs of the smoke and then returned the calumet to Mattahorn.

Mattahorn laid the calumet aside and addressed Governor Stuyvesant: "Great Sachem of the Dutch, welcome to the homeland of the Lenape and to our council fire." (Lasse Cock translated the greeting into Dutch.) Mattahorn continued. "The Lenape wish to become better acquainted with the Great Sachem of the Dutch and to determine his purpose for coming to our homeland with so many warriors, ships, and great guns.

"Great Sachem of the Dutch, we have observed that you are a brave and bold warrior of renown. Could you favor us with a story or two from your adventures? Especially tell us how you came to have the wooden leg with its silver bracelets."

"Sachem Mattahorn, Sachem Sinques, and Sachem Pemenetta," replied Stuyvesant, "I am honored to be your guest at this Lenape council fire along with Sander Boyer,[76] my interpreter, and Wilhelmus Grasmeer, a clergyman of the Holy Christian Church. Indeed, my wooden leg with its silver bracelets is a badge of courage I would rather not have,

[76] Three years later the Swedes branded Alexander (Sander) Boyer "an evil and ill-reputed man."

but one that I cannot hide or do without. (Here he patted his wooden leg affectionately.)

"Sachem Mattahorn, the story of my leg goes like this. I was born in Holland fifty-nine years ago. For many years the Spanish ruled the Netherlands very cruelly, but finally the Dutch people were able to drive off the Spanish from our homeland and rule ourselves. However, lasting hatred between the two countries continued, and the Dutch armies and sailors continued to attack Spanish shipping and colonies. At the age of forty-two I became part of an invading force that attacked and conquered the Spanish colony of Curacoa in the West Indies far to the south of here." At the mention of Curacoa, all three sachems leaned forward ever so slightly.

"In a few years I became governor of Curacoa," Governor Stuyvesant continued. "Our trade and the development of the island prospered while I was governor.

"Northeast of Curacoa lay another small island, St. Martin, controlled by the Portuguese. I decided to attack St. Martin and add it to our Dutch possessions. During the attack, a ball struck my leg and severed it from the limb. Not only was my leg lost, but we lost the battle as well. I was shipped back to the Netherlands, where my leg healed, and the doctors fitted me with this marvelous wooden leg. With it, I am a governor again. Without it, I am nobody. Three years after the battle, I arrived in New Amsterdam and have now been governor there for four years.

"Sachem Mattahorn, it is my intention to expand the Dutch trade and the colony of New Netherlands to include all the land here on the South River. Tell me, how much land have the Swedes bought from the sachems or chiefs of this river?"

"Great Sachem of the Dutch," answered Mattahorn, "truly the marvel of your wooden leg is an impressive thing. But I am thinking about other aspects of your tale. Tell me, were there any native people living on the island of Curacoa when you took it from the Spanish? What did these people do? Did they welcome the Dutch?"

"Yes, Great Sachem of the Lenape," replied Stuyvesant, "there were a few native people left on the island. Most of them had died under Spanish rule. We had to bring in many workers to work in the salt mines, the tobacco fields, and the cane fields, and to help with the shipping trade. These people really didn't care whether the Dutch or the Spanish ruled the island."

"Governor Stuyvesant," rejoined Mattahorn, his voice assuming a sharp, commanding edge, "tell me. Were all the workers you brought to Curacoa black slaves? Tell me. Did Governor Kieft send you any Mohican slaves from New Amsterdam? What has become of them? Tell me the truth."

"Sachem Mattahorn, I did not come to this council fire to make enemies but to make friends. I see that you are very wise and understand many things far beyond the lands of the Lenape River. For me to try to hide the truth from you would be foolish.

"You already know the answers to your questions. I cannot undo what Madman Kieft has done to the Lenape and the Mohicans. But I can tell you that Madman Kieft never made it to his home in Europe. The Almighty God has tried him and found him wanting. He went down with the ship that carried him back to the Netherlands for trial. I also can tell you that one of my first acts as governor of New Amsterdam was to forbid the sale of brandy to the Indians. The Dutch want to trade with the Lenape, not destroy them.

"Sachem Mattahorn, let us get on with the business for which I have come. How much land have the Swedes bought from the Lenape?"

"Governor Stuyvesant, all nations coming here are welcome. We sold land to the first ones who asked for it. Everyone knows that the Dutch were the earliest comers and discoverers."

"Sachem Mattahorn, you have evaded my question. How much land did you sell to the Swedes?"

"Governor Stuyvesant, when the Dutchman, Turn Coat Minuit, came to us on behalf of the Swedish Queen and wanted to buy land from us to build a house on, I made it as plain as the sun to him that he was welcome to build among us and trade among us if he would live peaceably and help protect the Lenape from the greedy Dutch. We sold him a patch of ground to build a house on and a plantation surrounded by six trees marked by turtles I carved on them with my own hand. Christina now stands on that plantation. The blankets we wear tonight are testimony of that sale. All the rest of the Swedish settlements have been made against our will and without our consent. Now the Swedes even prescribe laws for us to follow. It excites our wonder that we, the native owners, should not do with our own what we please. Furthermore, neither the Swedes nor any other nation have bought land from us as right owners, and neither we nor any other natives have received anything for it."

"Sachem Mattahorn, but did you not sell land on the Manayunk River[77] to my deputies three years ago? Are you sure you have not sold the land south of Christina to the Swedes?"

"Governor Stuyvesant, you do not understand. We did not sell land along the Manayunk River to your deputies. We do

---

[77] The Manayunk River is the Lenape name for the Schuylkill River flowing through Philadelphia, Penna. *Manayunk* means "Where we go to drink."

not sell land to the Dutch or any other nation. We only allow others to use the land with us. But why do you ask the same question so often? Did we not tell you that we have not sold the lands to the Swedes or to any other person?"

"Sachem Mattahorn, if you have not sold the land from Christina south to Swanendael on the west side of the Lenape River to any other person, will you now sell it to me?"

"Governor Stuyvesant, I must now remind you that one of the conditions for coming to our council fire was that you would be prepared to tell us the latitude of your warship anchored near the mouth of Neshaminy Creek. We now await your answer."

"Sachem Mattahorn, it is impossible for me to imagine why you need this information. Are you planning to take up sailing? Do your savages plan to capture my fleet and sell it to the Swedes? Nevertheless, I will give you the reading. It is just a few minutes over forty degrees latitude."

"Governor Stuyvesant, your question, 'Will we sell you the land south of Fort Christina?' requires that we sachems crawl through many thorny thickets before we can answer it. Please sit still until we return."

The three sachems withdrew from the council fire, and a lengthy talk ensued. The sachems discussed the problems.

How could the Lenape maintain friendly relations with the Dutch, whose past killings and ongoing alliance with the Mengwe called for revenge and defiance, not an alliance? And how could the Lenape maintain friendly relations with the Swedes if Big Belly found out they were selling land to the Dutch and trading with them instead of the Swedes? Suppose the Swedes again became strong enough to drive the Dutch out and punish the Lenape?

And if the mighty Dutch fleet now floating on the Lenape

River crushed the power of the Swedes, who would check the greedy Dutch from turning on the Lenape and swallowing them as they had their brethren, the Mohicans, at Drunk Island?

The night was nearly gone when the three sachems finally returned to the council fire and resumed their seats. All sat in silence for a long spell before Mattahorn rose to his feet and turned to face the east. With his back to those gathered around the fire, the sage spoke easily and clearly, addressing not only those gathered at the edge of the Neshaminy, but all the Lenape. His voice still rings through the forest today.

It is true. The Swede builds and plants, indeed, on our lands, without buying them or asking us. It is true that the Dutch and the English also take lands from us and build and plant on them.

All come to the River of the Lenape and wish to "buy a little land." We freely give the land to whoever asks, and in return they give gifts to us to secure our consent.

Soon we find that a little land is never enough. A bigger piece is never big enough. Each Christian nation and people wants ALL the land. The Swede cannot dwell in peace with the Dutch, and the Dutch cannot dwell in peace with the English, and none of them, ere long, dwell in peace with the Lenape.

The Lenape wish to dwell in peace with all who come to the Lenape River. We wish to share the land with them and to trade with them. And Christian nations who come must learn to live in peace with other Christian nations.

Therefore, we, the rightful owners of the lands

along the Lenape River, will not anger the Swedes by selling land to the Dutch. Perchance the Swedes shall again become strong and tear down the houses of the Dutch and the sacred poles marking their claims. Then the Swedes would be angry with the Lenape.

We do not wish to anger the Dutch by refusing to sell them land. Perchance the mighty army of the Dutch will destroy the Swedes, and then the Dutch will be angry with the Lenape.

Therefore, the Lenape will present to Governor Stuyvesant the land on the west side of the Lenape River from Suppeckongh to Canaresse[78] as a gift.

The condition of the gift is that the Dutch will dwell peaceably among us. The Dutch may build houses and trading posts on that land, but I, Sachem Mattahorn, along with Sachem Sinques and Sachem Pemenetta forbid the governor to drive the Swedes from among us. The Lenape wish both the Swedes and the Dutch to remain.

But if the Dutch have found the Lenape honeytree and intend to destroy the hive and rob the bees of their honey, it is only fitting that they should feel our stingers as well.

We will defend our homeland.

And be advised, O mighty Governor, if you drive the Swedes out in defiance of our warning, the King of England has already granted to a mighty English lord all the land on the South River as far north as forty degrees latitude. Live peaceably now with the Swedes and the Lenape, or you will rue the day when

---

[78] The land from the muddy river to the thickets. A portion of land along the Delaware River from the Christina south that included the land where Governor Stuyvesant built Fort Casimir.

you made enemies of your friends.

By the time Mattahorn had finished his discourse, the light of dawn had begun to push the darkness westward. Mattahorn remained motionless, silhouetted by the brightening sky. Standing tall and erect, he lifted his right arm upward with the index and middle finger extended, and began to chant:

Great Spirit,
Maker of the sky, the earth, the sun, the moon,
Keeper of the spirits of the fish, the birds, the animals, the
trees, the stones,
Guardian of the Four Winds,
Thank you for bringing light again to the People of the
Dawn.
Thank you for sending fire to warm our houses and cook our
food.
Thank you for bringing water to inspire the ground and to
quench our thirst.
Thank you for the ground to grow the maize and the deer to
give us meat.
For the ancient song of the Lenape,
For the everlasting sun that rises this day,
I, Mattahorn, the Great Sachem of the Lenni Lenape,
thank you.

When Mattahorn had finished his chant, he took a small pinch of tobacco from his pouch and sprinkled it on the ground before him. Then he stood motionless with his right arm still raised and his two fingers pointed upward.

No one knew exactly who gave the signal, but Mattahorn was still standing there when the warriors came and pointed the Dutch guests toward the waiting canoes. Strutting Turkey climbed into the lead canoe, carefully preened his dried-out garments, and then sailed off down the sun-drenched Neshaminy as proud of himself as a strutting turkey tom.

Exactly ten days later the same three canoes paddled past the council fire landing to a point one mile further up the Neshaminy to the village where a young sachem named Tamenand lived. There the warriors unloaded twelve coats of duffels, twelve kettles, twelve axes, twelve adzes, twenty-four knives, twelve bars of lead, and four guns with some powder.

Everyone understood. These were gifts from Strutting Turkey in exchange for the land Mattahorn had granted the Dutch.

Strutting Turkey loaded the supplies, great guns, and people from Fort Nassau on his ships. He demolished the fort. Then he sailed down the Lenape River to the newly built fort at the Sand Hook[79] just below Christina. There he unloaded the great guns and mounted them. This time he pointed the guns at the river. Now, no ship could pass by the new Fort Casimir unless the Dutch willed it.

Governor Stuyvesant's ships made prizes of any Virginian boats they caught sailing on the Lenape River and made them pay "recognition" or duty on all the goods they had sold the Swedes for four years past.

He did not attack the Swedes. He did tear down all the sacred poles the Swedes had erected along the Lenape River.

In the beginning of the month of roasting ears,[80] Strutting Turkey, master of the Lenape River, left two warships to patrol the Lenape River and returned with the rest of his fleet to New Amsterdam.

---

[79] The land just presented to Governor Stuyvesant by the Lenape sachems.

[80] Governor Stuyvesant completed Fort Casimir and returned to New Amsterdam August 1651.

The two warships returned to New Amsterdam before winter, leaving only the garrison at Fort Casimir to control the river for the Dutch. The Swedes received no goods from Sweden, and they could purchase only at very high prices from the Virginians. As a result, the Swedes had nothing to trade with the Lenape.

Even though the Lenape wished to trade with the Swedes, they had no choice but to trade with the Dutch. Big Belly kept promising the Lenape that a ship would soon arrive. He sent his own son, Gustaf Printz, home to plead for help. None came. Finally, two years after the first Dutch attacks, he called the Lenape to Printz Hall to renew their friendship. He gave out small gifts and promised them that a good stock of supplies would arrive in a few months, for he himself was going to the fatherland.

Only eight months after Big Belly left, another Swedish ship sailed up the Lenape River bearing supplies, colonists, and a new governor, Johan Rising.

On the way up the Lenape River, the ship stopped at Fort Casimir. Twenty-one houses now stood near Strutting Turkey's fort. Governor Rising found the fort and the houses protected by only nine Dutch soldiers and thirteen cannons. Besides, the soldiers' muskets were at the gunsmith's and there was no powder for the cannons. Newly arrived Governor Rising demanded the surrender of the fort and promised all liberty and good offers to the Dutch soldiers and inhabitants if they would give up without a fight. The Dutch said they didn't care who possessed the fort as long as they were allowed to dwell there safely and freely. Accordingly, the Dutch pulled down the red, white, and blue flag, and the Swedes raised one of their own blue and yellow flags over the fort. Then the ship carrying the new governor and the new master of the Lenape River sailed on up the river and docked at Fort Christina.

However, the Swedish settlers on the ship as well as the sailors were so weak from sickness they couldn't even row the boats to shore. The old settlers had to unload the ship. Sickness spread to the Lenape, so for a time the Lenape broke off all contact with the Swedes. This hurt the Swedes. With the coming of the ship, the number of people in the Swedish colony had increased from fifty to more than three hundred. The settlers badly needed to buy meat and fish from the Lenape.

The new governor invited the Lenape on the western bank of the Lenape River to a council at Printz Hall. Mattahorn, along with eleven other Lenape sachems and twenty followers, came to the council. The Swedish orator[81] spoke carefully and kindly on behalf of the Great Queen of Sweden.

"Great sachems of the Lenape and all who hear me this day. Remember the former friendship that existed between the Lenape and the Swedes from the day that Turn Coat Minuit first sailed up the Lenape River and with your consent founded Christina. We wish you to remember the kind words and the laws our Great Queen laid out to protect the natives of this fair land.

"Remember the kindness of Pastor Campanius and his love for you as he labored to teach you the joys of the Christian faith in your own tongue.

"And remember, if you will, the efforts of Governor Printz to protect you from the greedy Dutch.

"I want to assure you today that the Swedes wish to renew that old compact of friendship with you. If any bad man has given you suspicions that we have evil in mind against you, as

---

[81] Gregorius Van Dyck served as interpreter and speechmaker at the council on 17 June 1654.

some have whispered among you, do not believe such a one. But if you will make and keep such a treaty with us, we will keep it irrevocably.

"And if you can, remember the land which we bought from you. Will you keep the purchases intact?"

All the Lenape present, sachems and followers, answered with one sound, "Yes."

Then the Swedes gave to each sachem present one yard of frieze,[82] one kettle, one ax, one hoe, one knife, one pound of powder, one stick of lead, and six awl points. Each follower received only some of these items. After receiving the gifts, the sachems withdrew to take counsel about how they should answer the Swedes. When they returned to the hall, Sachem Hackeman spoke for the Lenape.

"Governor Rising, we see that a new and better day is beginning since you have come to us. Therefore, we shall call you Morning Light.

"Governor Morning Light, we see what good friends you are. You have given us such gifts. We have shamed ourselves that at times we have spoken evil of our friends and on occasion have even done you harm. Now," Hackeman promised as he stroked his left arm three times with his right hand, "we shall be special friends. If in the time of Governor Printz," the orator continued while striking his breast repeatedly, "our peoples have been as one body and one heart, hereafter they shall be as one head." Here Sachem Hackeman grasped his head with his hands and twisted his hands around as though tying a secure knot. "Furthermore," Sachem Hackeman continued, "as a calabash is a round growth without crack or break, hereafter we shall be as one head without a crack."

[82] Frieze was a rough, shaggy woolen cloth used for outer garments.

Now Sachem Hackeman again turned to his fellow Lenape and asked if he spoke for them all. Again the Lenape answered with one sound, "Yes."

Then the Swedes fired two of the great guns in a Swedish salute: *BOOM. BOOM.* And the Lenape fired their guns into the air, making a great noise.

After the noise quieted and the excitement faded, Hackeman pushed on. "From this day forward we will do the Swedes no harm, nor kill your people or your cattle. We will regard the enemies of the Swedes as our own enemies, and we will report any danger to the settlement we may by chance hear of. We will keep all the land purchases intact. In addition, the Swedes may build a house and fort at Passayunk[83] where the greatest number of us dwell.

"We are well satisfied with the Swedes," Hackeman continued. "Yet there is a problem. We have received sickness from the ship that brought you here, and we fear that all our people may perish. We have seen fire around the ship at night, and we believe that an evil spirit has come in the vessel. We have a great sachem, Teotacken, who lives at Siconece.[84] Could you not give us a boat that we might fetch Teotacken to drive this bad manito away? May Teotacken go down to the ship with his strong medicine and carry the spirit away?"

Governor Rising himself answered the request for a boat. "Yes," he agreed, "the sickness did come on the ship, for the Swedes also suffer from it. We wish we could tell you how to overcome this sickness. We cannot. But neither do we think Teotacken can drive the bad manito away. The Lord God controls everything, and He can heal you of the sickness. Put your trust in Him. He is stronger than all evil spirits.

[83] The land between the Schuylkill River and the Delaware River. In present day Philadelphia, PA.

[84] Called by the Dutch, "Swanendael" and "The Hoerenkill." Today Lewes, Delaware.

"Only yesterday I sent a boat down the river. Today I do not have another. So I cannot furnish you a boat I do not have to fetch Teotacken."

After the conclusion of the council, the Swedes fed the Lenape two large vessels of *sappan* and some strong drinks. I am sure the Swedes meant it well, Glikkikan, but strong drink tears the soul out of the Lenape. Perhaps it's true that there were no evil manitos on the ship. Perhaps there were evil manitos on the ship. Maybe yes. Maybe no. But we know there are evil manitos in the rum. Glikkikan, do not tempt those evil spirits, for they will destroy you.

Morning Light proved to be a good governor. He relaxed the harsh rules of Big Belly and allowed the Lenape to trade directly with the settlers. The Lenape could even sell land directly to the colonists. Morning Light allowed the sachems and all the Lenape to pass freely in and out of the forts and treated them with kindness and forbearance.

As for Mattahorn, he watched and pondered the situation. He knew it was only a matter of time until Strutting Turkey would return to the Lenape River. Doubtless, he would return with strong ships and many soldiers. Would Strutting Turkey retake only Fort Casimir? Or would he ignore Mattahorn's warning and drive the Swedes away as well?

Mattahorn met with Morning Light and talked about Strutting Turkey and the Dutch and the Mengwe. "Yes," Morning Light admitted, "Strutting Turkey will return, and he will not be humbled a second time. Just a month ago Strutting Turkey captured a Swedish supply ship that had mistakenly sailed past the Lenape River and on to New Amsterdam. He kept the ship and the cargo. But," Morning Light continued hopefully, "I think Sweden will force the Dutch to pay for the ship and cargo."

Pay for the ship and cargo? Hah! Glikkikan! The Dutch never paid the Swedes one turkey feather.

Morning Light and Mattahorn smoked slowly as they thought about the questions hanging over the Lenape homeland. At one of these councils, Falling Leaf appeared. Afterward, he quietly vanished unnoticed into the western forest. When Falling Leaf returned to Christina, he brought with him four Susquehannock sachems—Chakcorietchiaque, Svanahändäz, Waskanäquäz, and Sahagoliwatquaz—who indicated that they had important matters to present from their entire council. And indeed they did.

Svanahändäz spoke for the group and on behalf of the joint council of the Susquehannocks. After a long oration, Svanahändäz edged into the main business: "We have traded with the Swedes, the Dutch, and the English. We find the Swedes unlike the Long Knives from Virginia. The Virginians shoot the Indians down like rabbits wherever they find them.

"The Swedes trade fairly and honestly for our furs and skins, whereas the Dutch traders will cheat us whenever they can. The Dutch give guns to the Mengwe and empower them to steal our peltries. The Dutch then buy our stolen furs and skins from the Mengwe.

"We want the Swedes to be strong and to remain among us.

"Therefore we present to the Swedes all the land on the east side of the Virginia River, all the way from the beginning of Chakakitque Falls unto the end of Amisacken Falls,[85] a land of choice soil, endowed with beautiful fresh rivers, so that many thousands of families who might settle there can find their nourishment.

"We give you this land for an everlasting possession, the

---

[85] A block of land over sixty miles in length and thirty miles in breadth along the eastern shore of the Chesapeake Bay.

land with everything that might be upon it—woods, the ground, fish, birds, and animals ..." and Svanahändäz named a long list of the birds, fish, and animals in the land they were offering. With graphic signs and sounds, he made sure the Swedes could picture each one.

"We promise that when the Swedish people arrive there to settle the land, we will supply them with venison and maize for a year without any pay on the condition that we can buy from the settlers cloth, guns, and other goods that we now must purchase from the Hollanders and English. In addition, we want you to settle blacksmiths and tanners there who can make our guns and other things for good pay.

"As a sign of our authority to make this gift, we four sachems present you with twenty beaver furs of the best and highest quality."

The Swedes fixed up papers and the Susquehannock sachems placed their marks on the papers. The Swedes gave cloth and guns and kettles to the Susquehannocks. Then Svanahändäz took Morning Light by the hand and led him forward on the floor and said, "As I now lead you by the hand, thus we will bring your people into the country, 'and we will sustain you there and defend you against Indians and against 'Christian' enemies."

To seal the whole deal, the Susquehannocks fired their guns in the air and the Swedes fired two cannons: *Boom! Boom!* in a Swedish salute.

Aged Mattahorn sat quietly by and watched the whole of the proceedings. Not a person there except Morning Light and Falling Leaf could possibly have guessed that they all were willing partners in Mattahorn's plan to thwart Strutting Turkey.

The treaty between the Swedes and the Susquehannocks

took place in the fawn month.[86] Less than two months later, in the month of roasting ears, twenty-one-year-old Falling Leaf again dropped by to visit Mattahorn. His boyish and lithe manner, his firm blue eyes, his quick wit, and nimble tongue enabled him to trade with the Lenape, the Susquehannocks, the Swedes, the English, and even the Dutch. All trusted him. For along with his natural gifts, he possessed one rare trait that endeared him to all: he was honest.

Mattahorn greeted him quietly in the Lenape way and welcomed him into his lodge. The aged sachem and the young trader sat comfortably in quietness while the simple succotash and the succulent venison were prepared and served. The quietness and the warmth of friendship extended past the repast until a "wh-wh-wh-wh-o-o-o-o"[87] called from the nearby woods, followed by three calls in rapid succession—"we-ko-lis, we-ko-lis, we-ko-lis."[88]

At last Mattahorn spoke affectionately as though addressing his own son. "Falling Leaf, what brings you again to my wigwam? Is it more than the joy of seeing me once again?"

"Sachem Mattahorn, your face indeed thrills me, and your voice warms my heart. After traveling through a den of rattlesnakes, one must always be glad to relax in the fox's lair."

Mattahorn waited before asking, "Falling Leaf, how did you come to travel through a den of rattlesnakes?"

"Sachem Mattahorn, I needed to do some trading business in New Amsterdam." Here Falling Leaf broke into a boyish grin and he winked at Mattahorn.

"Trading business?" queried Mattahorn.

Falling Leaf shrugged. "Anyway, I was in New Amsterdam,

[86] The council took place 6 June 1655.

[87] The call of the great horned owl.

[88] The Lenape name and call of the whippoorwill.

and I have come here straightway. The rattlesnake lies coiled
and ready to strike. Strutting Turkey has gathered together
a fleet of seven ships. Five ships have at least four cannons
each. A mighty warship with forty cannons has just arrived
from Holland carrying more than two hundred soldiers
and sailors. The Dutch call the ship *De Waag*, meaning "the
balance scale," such as we use in trading. Strutting Turkey also
demands that trading ships join the fleet even if the owner
does not want to. Then he forces men to join as soldiers, and
if they will not, he forces them to pay a tax to support the
attack."

Again Mattahorn waited before asking, "Falling Leaf, what
makes you sure that Strutting Turkey is preparing to come to
the Lenape River?"

"Sachem Mattahorn, it had been widely proclaimed
throughout New Amsterdam that a particular day was to
be set aside as a day of prayer and fasting to invoke God's
blessing on the expedition. Thinking this service could prove
both interesting and entertaining, I gave in to my curiosity
and attended service on the appointed day. Besides, I can
always use an extra blessing from God. I was not let down.

"Sachem Mattahorn, do you remember the preacher
Strutting Turkey brought along to the council fire? His name
was Wilhelmus Grasmeer. You and I call him Bent Stick. In
the midst of the service I attended, Bent Stick got up and
prayed on and on like a babbling brook. He prayed to his
God and asked Him to grant the fleet complete safety on
their journey to the South River. He prayed for favorable
winds and calm seas. He asked that God would turn aside
the bullets of the Swedes from the Dutch soldiers. Bent Stick
prayed that the Dutch soldiers might be able to subdue the
cruel savages who attack Christians in the most treacherous

ungodly manner. And Bent Stick asked God to hear their cry and assist the Dutch in obtaining the return of the lands and possessions unjustly stolen from them on the South River, and if it please the Almighty God, to grant the Dutch force a complete victory so that all nations might know that good has triumphed over evil and thus His name shall be glorified.

"Sachem Mattahorn, there is no doubt about the intentions of Strutting Turkey. Remember Curacoa."

"Yes, Falling Leaf, I shall long remember Curacoa. The time has come for us to act. You shall go yet this night and warn Morning Light of the gathered fleet and of Strutting Turkey's intentions. We will need the help of the Susquehannocks, so I will send another messenger in search of Sachem Svanahändäz. Then we will wait for the fleet."

Falling Leaf slipped easily off into the night to find Morning Light. And when the light of dawn flushed the eastern sky, another messenger sped westward bearing a long black belt of wampum.

This was the message of the black wampum belt:

> To Sachem Svanahändäz, the Great Sachem of the Susquehannocks. From Mattahorn the Great Sachem of the Lenni Lenape. A great danger has arisen to the Swedes. Strutting Turkey has prepared a large fleet to attack and destroy the Swedes on the Lenape River. If you would be the "Protectors of the Swedes," as you claim to be, now is the time to take up the hatchet. Gather a force of two hundred of your best warriors and prepare them for the trail to Drunk Island. I will notify you when the fleet and the soldiers have arrived in our homeland. Guard yourselves against

the Mengwe. When I send word, travel swiftly to the outlying area close to Drunk Island where the Dutch settlers and Mengwe have been killing the Mohicans. The Dutch soldiers will be gone. Arrive at night. Kill one hundred men. Do no harm to women or children. Return quickly to your homes and leave no traces behind.

Sachem Svanahändäz listened to the message. Then he repeated the message. At the end he reached out his hand, took the long black wampum belt from the messenger, and said simply, "Tell Sachem Mattahorn that we will be ready for the signal."

Two weeks after the special day of fasting and prayer, Strutting Turkey sailed into the bay with his seven-ship fleet led by the warship, *De Waag*.[89] Three days after entering the bay, the fleet sailed right past the guns of the fort Morning Light had taken from the Dutch. The Swedes were at the cannons, and every boat in the fleet sailed past within range of the guns, but the commander never gave the order to fire.

The Lenape were watching.

Glikkikan, maybe it was not a lack of bravery on the part of the Swedes that held back the shooting. Maybe it was common sense. Counting the sailors and soldiers, there must have been seven or eight hundred men, and all the ships together carried fifty-four cannons. But, Glikkikan, if people will not strike a spark in their own defense, it is hard for anyone else to hold their cause.

Once above the Swedish fort on the Sand Hook, the fleet stopped and landed the Dutch troops. Strutting Turkey demanded the surrender of the fort he had built.

[89] The fleet entered the Delaware Bay 6 September 1655, but a tide and a calm prevented him from proceeding up the river until the following day.

Mattahorn waited no longer. He sent the signal west to
Svanahändäz. Revenge for the slave trade and the murders
of their Mohican brethren was an old score that had to be
settled. Then the Lenape waited to see what would happen
next in the contest for control of their homeland.

The Swedes hauled down their flags, and the Dutch raised
theirs once again over Fort Casimir on the Sand Hook.
Strutting Turkey and his forces went into the reclaimed
fort and celebrated divine services.[90] Bent Stick prayed and
thanked God for the victory.

Then Strutting Turkey moved his forces against Christina
itself. The two warships closed the river to traffic, and soldiers
built trenches and mounted cannons all around the city.
Dutch soldiers overran the farms above Christina River,
killing the cattle, swine, and goats of the settlers, breaking
open the houses and plundering everything they could get at.
The Dutch soldiers invaded Printz Hall on Tinicum Island
and carried off property which settlers had stored there for
safekeeping.

The plight of the Swedes increased daily, and in the middle
of the autumnal month[91] Morning Light surrendered all of
New Sweden to Strutting Turkey.

Glikkikan, the Swedes had not fired one shot in self-
defense. Instead, the Swedes made a parade out of the
surrender. Thirty soldiers marched out of the fort beating
their drums, playing fifes, flying banners, burning matches,
holding musket balls in their mouths, and shooting their side
arms.

What brave men they were! They cared not for honor nor
treaties nor for the Lenape enough to fire one ball, but only

---

[90] Took place 2 September 1655 by the Dutch calendar.

[91] The Swedes surrendered to the Dutch 15 September 1655.

for their flags and sacred poles. If they had fired but one cannon, the Lenape were ready. If the Swedes had fired but ten shots, the Lenape would have swarmed out like angry bees to sting the backsides of the Dutch soldiers. Dutch cannons and guns were pointed at the fort, and the backs of Dutch soldiers would have been easy marks for the arrows of any Lenape warrior. In darkness a sharpened tomahawk is always better than a gun. In trees and swamps, the Dutch would have been as helpless as a deer on river ice.

But the Swedes did nothing. Nothing. And so the Lenape did nothing. It was better to trade with the victor than to madden the victor by fighting for a loser.

Falling Leaf found out that Strutting Turkey did not receive word of the raid at Drunk Island until the day before the Swedes gave up New Sweden. The raid had been a success. Following Mattahorn's instructions, the Susquehannocks had killed one hundred men in nine hours and disappeared. Some suspected the Lenape on the South River had done it in revenge for the attack on the Swedes, but no one was certain.[92]

At any rate, less than one-half hour after the Swedes paraded out of the fort, Strutting Turkey with all his officers and entire council appeared at the fort and offered to make a league with the Swedes.

"The country is large enough for both the Swedes and the Dutch," he told Morning Light. "If you will allow the Dutch to dwell undisturbed below the Christina River and in possession of the land there, the Swedes may keep all their possessions north of the fortress. We will allow the present troubles to be forgotten and forgiven," he offered.

Not knowing of the raid that had caused such a turnabout

[92] Johnson, Amandus, The Swedes on the Delaware, Philadelphia, PA, 1927, p. 331.

in Strutting Turkey's position, Morning Light and his officers turned down the offer with one voice. Their reasoning went like this. They were not ready to give up their claims for the damages done by the attacks. They could not subsist in the country because their provisions were gone. A great part of their cattle and swine were killed, and many of the plantations laid to waste. Finally, it would be disgraceful to their superiors to reoccupy the fort.

Glikkikan, I guess Morning Light never thought of asking the Lenape and Susquehannocks for food and provisions. The Swedes must not have thought anything about the danger to the Lenape or their generous offer from the Susquehannocks. All they cared about was their so-called honor.

I guess Morning Light and his officers never thought of asking Strutting Turkey to replace their losses and grant them new provisions. The Swedes thought they lacked guns and men and supplies. What they lacked was courage. Strutting Turkey's offer to Morning Light shows it would have been possible for the Swedes to have coexisted with the Dutch. If the Swedes had only fired the first great gun, if they had followed it with a few more volleys, if they had called on the Lenape, Strutting Turkey would surely have gone home with his feathers badly mussed.

As it was, for we dare not glory in what might have been, only a few handfuls of Swedes decided to stay in their homes and pledge their loyalty to the Dutch rulers. The rest of the Swedes sailed off aboard the *De Waag*, still grumbling about the injustices and losses they had suffered at the hands of the Dutch. The entire fleet departed the Lenape River in the middle of the harvest month[93] only six weeks after its arrival.

[93] The fleet departed 11 October 1655.

Strutting Turkey's conquest left the Lenape and the Susquehannocks stirred like the winds of a great storm. Strutting Turkey had defied Mattahorn's condition[94] for the gift of land and removed the Swedes as a counterbalance to Dutch power. In addition, this mastery allowed the Dutch monopoly status of the fur trade, and therefore all trade, along the Lenape River.

Clearly, the Lenape homeland was threatened by the advance of a greedy foe who had proved his intent ever since coming to Drunk Island. I imagine Strutting Turkey knew he had beat on the Lenape hornets' nest with a club and left the whole South River buzzing. But what could the Lenape do about it? Maybe Strutting Turkey decided to leave the Lenape alone for several months. Maybe he thought that by the next year's trapping season things would be calmed down and the past forgotten.

The winter passed, and the following spring, while the whales still spouted in the bay, a Swedish supply ship bearing 110 settlers and a good stock of supplies sailed into the boiling pot along the Lenape River.[95] Neither the passengers nor the crew knew about the Dutch takeover of New Sweden until they sailed up in front of Fort Casimir and saw the red, white, and blue Dutch flag flying. The ship stopped before the fort, and two old hands from the beginning days of New Sweden went ashore.[96]

The Lenape excitedly reported the blue flag with its yellow crossbars waving atop the masts of the new ship. Word spread quickly along the Lenape River, and Swedes and Lenape alike prepared for the wondrous arrival. Settlers had come. Supplies

---

[94] The condition for the land gift was that the Dutch must live peaceably with the Swedes.

[95] The ship, the *Mercurius*, arrived at Fort Casimir 13 March 1656.

[96] Hendrick Huygen, a nephew of Peter Minuit, and Johan Papegoja, the son-in-law of Johan Printz.

had come. Trade goods had come.

However, the ship remained anchored below Fort Casimir. The Dutch arrested Hendrick Huygen as an enemy of the people and denied Johan Papegoja permission to proceed up the river and unload his passengers and cargo. The Dutch commander and Papegoja both sent reports to New Amsterdam. Stutting Turkey replied, "The ship will be allowed to return to Sweden unmolested and she may stop at New Amsterdam to take on additional supplies. But she is NOT allowed to unload on the South River."

Twelve soldiers accompanied the missive back to the Lenape River to help quell any uprising of the Swedes. The soldiers were to compel all Swedes who had not yet sworn loyalty to the Dutch crown to do so now. Falling Leaf along with two other Swedes were designated as "undesirable citizens" because they held secret conferences with the Indians who often came to their homes, and as usual, were well received. These undesirables along with those who refused to swear loyalty were to be brought to New Amsterdam where they could be watched more closely.

Falling Leaf laughed when he told Mattahorn of the seriousness of his misconduct. "I have committed great sins," he mocked. "I have befriended the Lenape and the Susquehannocks and treated them with dignity and honor. Surely the wrath of God will fall upon me."

Falling Leaf knelt down on the floor of the lodge, carefully folded his hands together, and implored of Mattahorn, "Please ask Bent Stick to pray for me that I might have my sins forgiven."

This was too much for even stoic Mattahorn. He smiled. "Get up," he commanded. "Give your burden to the Great Spirit, for he smiles upon kindness and goodness for the red man, and," he added thoughtfully, "upon the white man as well."

Falling Leaf rose to his feet. "Sachem Mattahorn," he said, "Johan Papegoja has decided to go himself to New Amsterdam and appeal the decision on the ship. I must accompany him, and I think it would be wise to have a silent escort of twenty warriors so that there be no mishaps along the way. Are there twenty warriors of courage among the Lenape who will serve as 'Protectors of the Swedes'?"

"Aye, my son," Mattahorn responded. "There be ten times twenty Lenape warriors, and more, who will never forsake a friend such as you. Nor will they forget the wrongs done by Dutch soldiers and their commanders against the Swedes and the Mohicans. You shall have your escort. And when you and Commander Papegoja return, we will take the ship and bring it to Fort Christina, if it is the last thing I do. Be careful in the rattlesnake den, and the Lenape will be ready to take the ship when you return."

When Falling Leaf and Commander Papegoja returned from the overland trip to New Amsterdam, they brought alarming news. The council had again forbidden the ship to unload its passengers and cargo and had also warned them that at the first favorable wind, they would dispatch the *De Waag* to enforce the departure order on the *Mercurius*.

That was enough for Mattahorn. "Falling Leaf," he said, "the time has again come to act. We are going to take over the *Mercurius*, sail it past the Dutch fort, and unload the provisions and our Swedish friends on Tinicum Island."

Falling Leaf gasped in wonder. Had the old chief lost his mind? "Most noble sachem, how will we do this?" he asked. "'Tis not a light thing to defy the guns of the Dutch.

Mattahorn spoke carefully. "Falling Leaf, here is what we

will do. The Lenape and the Susquehannocks will call 1,000 warriors into the woods behind Fort Casimir.

"You are a Swede. Your countrymen and your friends depend on you. You must go into the fort and persuade the commander to release Hendrick Huygen and to surrender the fort. If he does not agree to your terms, we will destroy it. The night is dark, and the small garrison in the fort cannot possibly defend it.

"Then we will sail the *Mercurius* up the river and unload it. Hendrick Huygen and none of the other Swedes will be responsible for this act of piracy. We, the Lenape, forced them to do it."

"But what about the *De Waag?*" Falling Leaf asked. "What if she arrives before we take over the *Mercurius?*"

"Falling Leaf," Mattahorn answered, "I have pondered that. If the *De Waag* arrives, you and the commander of the Dutch Fort Casimir must board the ship and run it aground. There is no other way."

The next morning Lenape messengers sprang into the woods. In two days time a few strong blue-eyed Swedes and hundreds of sullen Lenape warriors drifted down the Lenape River. Many paddled upstream from the south. Others came overland, but they all camped inland just far enough to be out of any danger from ship cannon.

The Dutch commander[90] nervously watched the many warriors traveling openly past the fort. He wondered what it all meant ... but not for long. Late one afternoon a lone Swede appeared at the fort and asked to speak to Commander Jacquet.[97] It was none other than Falling Leaf. He was hurriedly admitted into the fort and granted audience with

[97] Jean Paul Jacquet served the West India Company many years in Brazil before coming to the Delaware as vice-director and magistrate. He took command on 8 December 1655, only five months before the events portrayed here.

the commander.

"Tell me," Commander Jacquet ordered, "who are you and what brings you here?"

"I am Lasse Cock and I have come to negotiate the passage of the *Mercurius* past the fort," Lasse said in his carefree way. It was as though such a stupendous request was simply a small favor he might ask of another trader.

"Lasse Cock!" Jacquet exploded. "I have orders to arrest you on sight and send you back to New Amsterdam. And what makes you think that I might even consider a direct countermand of my express orders? Besides, the *De Waag* is already on the way to enforce Governor Stuyvesant's orders."

"Commander Jacquet, I know what your orders are," Lasse replied calmly. "I can inform you that the *De Waag* has been sighted in the bay. I am also sure that you have seen the many painted warriors coming to the fort. They have come to take the fort and silence its cannons. I am sure it would be in your best interest to negotiate with me."

"Ah, Falling Leaf! we will certainly talk, but you must remember that you are now my prisoner and will be delivered to New Amsterdam on the De Waag."

Falling Leaf shrugged. "I am not sure who is whose prisoner, but I am willing to show you your choices."

The two seated themselves in the bare room and Commander Jacquet poured himself a small glass of brandy. Falling Leaf leaned back in his chair and with a gentle smile asked, "Commander Jacquet, is it ever right to disobey orders?"

Jacquet looked steadily into the calm blue eyes of the powerful young man standing before him. He saw a hardened courage there born of confidence in the truth and the rightness of his cause.

Jacquet shuddered slightly and his eyes dropped. "I will negotiate," he said. "I will release Henrick Huygen and deliver him to the Mercurius while you can still see him set aboard the ship. And if you fail me, you will stay with me as a prisoner to be delivered to New Amsterdam."

Lasse Cock shrugged. "Would you have a drink and a chair with a view of the ship that we might relax while Master Huygen is transferred to the boat?" he asked.

Falling Leaf carefully studied the fort while Jacquet busied himself arranging the prisoner's release. When Jacquet once more seated himself and had helped himself to a small glass of brandy, Falling Leaf leaned back on his chair and with a gentle smile asked, "Commander Jacquet, is it ever right to disobey orders?"

"I can think of no time when it would be right to disobey orders," Jacquet said thoughtfully, "for if I could disobey my superior when I thought best, then those under me would also be free to disobey me whenever they thought best. The whole chain of command would break down."

"So what if your superior issues a bad order? What if you know it is wrong to do what he has ordered you to do? Is your conscience dead when the King speaks? Does guilt never haunt you and taunt you when you have done an evil thing?"

"Lasse Cock, you are indeed clever. First you would suggest that I should disobey my orders. Then you intimate that guilt dogs my life. And now you wish to play with my conscience. My orders are the burden that another man's conscience must bear, be he king or priest. My own hands are clean and my conscience unsullied when carrying out my orders. But the demons of guilt do taunt me. That I cannot deny."

"Commander Jacquet, I take it that if your orders told you to march straight into hell, you would obey. And when you arrived there, you would say, 'I was only obeying orders.'

"Commander Jacquet, listen to me," Falling Leaf continued. "Right and wrong are not determined by commanders, governors, kings, or priests. Neither Governor Stuyvesant nor Clergyman Grasmeer can alter right or wrong any more than he can change the coming and going of the tide or the rising and the setting of the sun. Neither can you escape the true knowledge of right and wrong, for each man has that knowledge within himself. When each man disobeys that knowledge of right or wrong, he must bear the nagging burden of guilt with him."

"Lasse Cock, I told you before that the demons of guilt taunt me. Is there no salve for a wounded spirit?"

"Yes, go and sin no more. Do not go to hell by obeying orders. Let us step outside now and walk along the edge of the fort so we can better see the *Mercurius*."

The two men moved to the outer wall of the fort and stood on the platform next to a protruding cannon. With the sinking sun behind them they commanded a stunning view of the *Mercurius* and the flowing river.

As the two stood there studying the river, the fort, and the ship, Falling Leaf asked innocently, "Commander Jacquet, were you on one of the ships when the Dutch sailed past this fort to take it from the Swedes?"

"Yes, I was one of the soldiers on the *De Waag*. That is an awesome warship," Jacquet replied.

"Did the *De Waag* sail within range of the cannon from the fort?" Falling Leaf probed.

"Yes, every ship in the fleet sailed within range of the fort's cannon. Why do you ask? Not a shot was fired," Jacquet protested.

Falling Leaf continued his interrogation undeterred.

"What would Strutting Turkey, ah, excuse me, Governor Stuyvesant have done if the cannon had fired upon the *De Waag* or any of the other smaller ships in the fleet? Could you have destroyed the fort by firing cannons from the ships? Yes, you probably could have inflicted some damage on the fort from the ship's cannon, but would not the ships have been at far greater risk of loss than the fort if the Swedes had fired back? Would it not have been impossible to take the fort without landing soldiers and storming the fort at some point? And what if, when the soldiers landed, they had found the woods filled with 1,000 maddened savages thirsting for revenge? Could the soldiers have escaped with their lives?"

Commander Jacquet studied his questioner and thought on the succession of questions. "Lasse Cock, I believe you are right," Jacquet said slowly. "The Dutch could not have taken this fort without landing soldiers if the Swedes had put up a fight. But were there 1,000 maddened savages waiting to attack the soldiers when they landed?"

"Commander Jacquet," Falling Leaf said very quietly, almost too quietly, "the other time, there were no savages waiting outside the fort because the Swedes did not fire the first bullet. This night there are 1,000 maddened savages outside the fort. They are angered because Strutting Turkey defied the Lenape condition set upon him that he allow the Swedes to live here. They have been driven crazy by the fear that they will be at the mercy of the cruel and greedy Dutch who will swallow them as the snake swallows the rat."

"Let us go inside, for the darkness has come upon us," Jacquet suggested. Once inside, with a small light burning in the sparsely furnished room, Jacquet asked, "So what are you telling me, Falling Leaf? What do you want to negotiate?"

"Commander Jacquet, do you know what happened at Swanendael?" Jacquet nodded and Falling Leaf continued. "I will tell you plainly. Tonight this fort lies solely at the kind mercies of 1,000 maddened Lenape whom 'Christians' call savages. Either you agree to allow the *Mercurius* to pass upstream unharmed with all aboard or the fort will be fired by dawn and everyone in it killed. And the killing will not stop with those in the fort, but death will be awarded to every Dutchman who lands on the South River to fight, to settle, or to trade. Commander Jacquet, could you not find enough kindness in your heart to avert such bloodshed?"

"Yes! Yes! My heart is indeed big enough to save my own skin," Jacquet replied sarcastically. "But how do I know you are not the biggest fraud ever reared in the wilds of this wilderness? How do I know there really are 1,000 maddened savages prowling outside the fort?"

"Commander Jacquet, that is a logical question. Are you sure that you want proof?"

"Aye, I will risk it," Jacquet muttered.

"Then we will step outside again for a moment," Falling Leaf suggested.

Falling Leaf stepped outside and listened quietly. Then he threw back his head and screamed the hunting cry of the panther.

Jacquet blanched and jumped backward. "I could swear you were murdering my mother," he cried.

Falling Leaf held up his hand. "Silence," he commanded.

From the woods beyond the fort and from the fields and houses surrounding the fort, hundreds of screams of dying women tore into the windy night. The screams continued, shattering the night, overlapping one another, and joining one another in a seemingly unending cry of death. Jacquet clutched at the wall for support. Suddenly Falling Leaf threw his head back once more and uttered another piercing scream. The fearful cries stopped.

"Shall we return into the blockhouse?" Jacquet asked anxiously. His voice quavered.

"Jacquet, do you not like the hunting cry of the panther?" Falling Leaf teased. "Perhaps 'tis only a group of cats hunting in the woods. Perhaps the west wind has only distorted the cries beyond all recognition."

Jacquet opened the door and sprang inside. "Stop your sport, Lasse Cock. Stop it. You would extort from me the wages of my past sins and dangle my conscience from a slender strand of truth. I cannot bear it. Demon, haunt me no more. Oh 'tis good the ghouls hunt outside the fort this night. My mouth is dry. I shall have another shot of brandy."

Falling Leaf stepped back and watched Jacquet closely as he raised the trembling glass to his lips. After he had drained half the glass, Jacquet extended the glass toward Falling Leaf and offered him a drink. In that moment a shaft shot through the still-open door, shattered the glass, and stuck itself into the opposite wall. Jacquet crashed to the floor. "The fiends are inside the fort," he gasped.

Falling Leaf took Jacquet by the hand and raised him to his feet. Jacquet tottered a bit and reached unsteadily for another glass of brandy. Falling Leaf waited while Jacquet drained the glass, then ordered, "Come, there is some work that must be done if the fort is to be saved and tragedy avoided." Jacquet obeyed, stumbling along in the direction Falling Leaf gently pushed him.

After that, doors opened and strong red men eased into the fort. They carried heavy bags of powder and lead shot out of storage and placed them in dugout canoes and small boats.

Five barrels of beer vanished. Red men pitched cannonballs over the edge of the fort and heard them splash into the river. Then the boats disappeared into the night.

After the last Indian boat had passed into the night, another sizable Dutch boat manned by Indians pushed out into the Lenape River. Aboard were Falling Leaf, Commander Jacquet, and Henrick Huygen.

The boat headed directly to the *Mercurius.* Someone threw a rope ladder down to Henrick and he climbed aboard to resume command of his ship. Then the boat drifted downstream with the current toward the bay and the mighty *De Waag* with its 40 cannons.

Dawn came to the Lenape River. The *Mercurius* stirred with great activity. Sailors bustled about arranging ropes, hoisting sails, and getting ready to lift anchor. Passengers who had waited so long to get off the boat cleaned and dressed as best they could. Canoes and boats kept shuttling back and forth from the western shore bringing Lenape and Swedes until another 110 passengers crowded on the deck.

I, Owechela, was there too. I got my wish. I climbed high up in the crow's nest on the main mast. Far, far below I watched miniature people hustling about. I saw the wind billowing the sails and the river rushing along. Clouds scooted eastward across the sky far above the blue flag with its yellow crossbars that fluttered proudly above my head. It was all like a dream.

I could hear the calls, the commands, and the cheers drifting up from the deck below. What a day. We, the Lenape, were taking over this great ship. It was true. I could see the great guns poking their ugly snouts through the holes in the fort, and I knew that we had to sail past them. I had no idea how we would get safely past, but to my young mind, it didn't matter. The Lenape were a great people. We were acting together, 1,000 strong. We would teach the Dutch a lesson. We would defend our homeland. As I lay there dreaming, nestled in the basket, it seemed I could hear again that ancient cry of the Lenape, "We carry the Spirit of Tamenend to the Land of the Dawn." My skin tingled, and I knew that everything would be all right.

Then I looked far to the south and jerked up with a start. A great ship sailed up the river toward us. I shouted, "Ship coming!" Everyone peered downriver. But no one else could yet see beyond the distant bend in the Lenape River. I watched anxiously. Soon I could make out the red, white, and blue stripes of the Dutch flag. "Dutch ship," I shouted to the worried throng below. And then she rounded the distant bend. Cannon bristled out the sides of the mighty warship as she sped toward us under full sail. I recognized her at once. It was none other than the awesome warship Strutting Turkey had used to frighten the Swedes into surrender only six months ago. "*De Waag,*" I shouted.

But I didn't have to tell anyone now. "*De Waag. De Waag. De Waag,*" broke out in anguished cries on the ship below. My heart sank. Had we come so close to taking the *Mercurius* only to lose it all again? I wondered. It seemed to me that the *De Waag* would soon be within firing range. Why were we not yet moving? Why did sailors not lift anchor and flee while there was still time? Instead, all activity on the ship stopped. It was as though the Lenape and the Swedes lay helplessly paralyzed under the spell of the snake's eyes. Were we indeed but a songbird falling helplessly into the jaws of the snake?

As I watched and trembled, a strange thing happened. As I said, the *De Waag* sped toward us under full sail. Suddenly she veered toward the east shore and the strong west wind drove her quickly onto a sandbar. The mighty warship shuddered and then stopped.

Two long dugout canoes manned by five Lenape warriors shot out at once from the bank on the eastern shore. Two men dropped quickly from the warship, one into each canoe. The one carrying Falling Leaf clung to the eastern shore as it pushed upstream. The other canoe swung toward the west bank carrying Commander Jacquet toward Fort Casimir.

When the canoe bearing Falling Leaf neared the eastern shore slightly above the spot where the *Mercurius* lay anchored, five more canoes paddled quietly out from the cover along the shoreline. In the lead canoe sat Mattahorn. Adorned in his red blanket given him by Turn Coat Minuit, here a dash of gold, there the bands of silver, the black scarf, the long gray hair dangling to his shoulders, and the tortoise creeping upward across his chest, there sat the venerable sachem, calm, wise, and proud.

Falling Leaf's canoe fell in beside Mattahorn's, and the two canoes followed by the other four paddled slowly toward us. A drumbeat on the shore kept time for the paddlers. And then the cry started, "We carry the Spirit of Tamenend in the Land of the Dawn." Over and over the cry swept across the Lenape River until the escort reached the *Mercurius*.

What a thrill! Our white sails held taut by the wind. The warmth of the spring morning. The color of the budding trees, the dark river, the beat of the drum, and the voices of the shouting Lenape drifting high up to me.

The canoes came in above the ship and paddled slowly around the boat until Mattahorn's canoe reached the side. The drum stopped. A sling dropped down to the canoe, and Mattahorn climbed in. Strong hands lifted him aboard the *Mercurius*. Falling Leaf clambered up the ladder and made his way to Mattahorn's side. He wrapped his strong right arm around the sachem's shoulder and the sachem placed his left arm over the shoulder of the powerful young Swede. Together they climbed to the poop deck above the captain's cabin. There, allowing Falling Leaf to steady him, Mattahorn looked out over his beloved homeland and extended his right hand above the horizon.

The crew lifted the anchor and the *Mercurius* surged forward,[98] free at last. Two cannons from the *Mercurius* boomed a Swedish salute, *BOOM. BOOM,* and one cannon responded from Fort Casimir with a pathetic *bum.* One would have thought maybe they were a bit low on powder. Braves in three canoes on each side of the *Mercurius* paddled furiously, seeing if they could outdistance the ship. Lined up along the edges of the ship stood a Swede and a Lenape, a Swede and a Lenape, a Swede and a Lenape. As the ship sailed past the fort, the captain swinging the ship purposely close by the fort, each Lenape reached out over the edge and stroked his left arm three times in that Lenape expression of special warmth. The watching Dutch lining the fort and the shores waved back.

The racing canoes fell further and further behind. Fort Casimir dropped out of sight. Mattahorn and Falling Leaf stood together on the poop deck as the ship pushed forward. And I, Owechela, floated along in the surreal clouds tasting the elixir of victory.

> *Glikkikan. Remember:*
> *'Tis not the size of the gun*
> *That will make men run,*
> *But the courage of those who tire,*

[98] Around 28 April 1656.

When the time has come to FIRE!

'Tis not the King's might
That determines the right,
But the truth men most admire,

When the time has come to FIRE!
'Tis not the guns of the King
That will make truth ring,
But the courage of those who inspire,
When the time has come to FIRE!

Narrated by Glikkikan

"Glikkikan, we got away with it," Owechela continued the next day. The story of the taking of the *Mercurius* had tired him out.

To him and to me the story had been so real. So vivid. So intense. There had been that day of triumph when the glory of my people shone through the haze and glittered on our hearts.

For although Owechela had not yet told me, I already knew that a suffocating weight pressed down upon the chest of the Lenape, making it hard to breathe the air around us. And that one deep gulp from the fresh air of a past victory had invigorated us both.

This morning I could see Owechela was rested and anxious to continue. His black eyes searched out mine and fixed upon them. It was as though Owechela wanted to pour his life and everything he dreamed into me. Nothing else mattered then—

the wigwam, Neshaminy Creek, the dogs, the deer, the forest, the settlers, the sun, the spirits—nothing, just the story.

"Go on," I urged. "Tell me what Strutting Turkey did when Mattahorn and Falling Leaf outsmarted him."

Chapter 8 – 1657

Mattahorn and Destiny

As told by Owechela

Strutting Turkey pretty much left things alone after
that. The *Mercurius* sailed on to Tinicum Island and
unloaded the settlers there.

Commander Jacquet reported to Strutting Turkey. He told
of the horrible threats the savages had made to kill all the
Dutch because of their attacks on the Swedes, and of how
his own brave actions on the Lenape River had averted a
terrible tragedy. He begged Strutting Turkey to overlook any
wrongdoing on the part of the Swedes, and even to ask the aid
of the Swedes in quieting the hornets' nest of savages on the
South River.

How do I know what Commander Jacquet reported to
Strutting Turkey? Falling Leaf had to accompany Hudde,
Jacquet's messenger, to New Amsterdam to ensure that the
Lenape didn't destroy him on the way.

The council at Drunk Island, headed of course by Strutting
Turkey, commended Commander Jacquet, excused all the
Swedes involved in the taking of the *Mercurius,* and even asked

if the Swedes would not help settle the differences between the savages and the Christians.

According to his orders, Commander Jacquet sent the *Mercurius* down the Lenape River to assist the *De Waag* in getting off the sandbar. Can you imagine that, Glikkikan? A Swedish merchant ship being asked to pull the mighty *De Waag* off a sandbar. I wish I could have seen that.

Then the Dutch took gifts off the *De Waag*, put them on the *Mercurius*, and in the name of the Dutch, the Swedes gave out gifts to the Lenape. Lots of them. Thus outward calm was restored once more between the Lenape and the Dutch.

Commander Jacquet had to pay. Only a year or so after the *Mercurius* sailed free, Strutting Turkey arrested Jacquet and threw him out of office because of unspecified complaints against him.[99] But we knew what the problem with Jacquet was: he had disobeyed orders.

Understand, Glikkikan, at times doing what is right may cost you a good bit, as it did Jacquet, but the price of a clean heart is always cheap.

The Lenape buried Mattahorn shortly after he sailed up the Lenape River for the last time. I can see him yet standing on the *Mercurius* with his arm outstretched over the homeland of the Lenape—a sage, a seer, a sachem, a savior—ah, a great man. From the moment of his death, women specially designated for the purpose raised a great cry through the village, "He is no more! He is no more!" Runners broke out immediately to carry the message to distant villages, "He is no more."

Hundreds made their way to his wigwam by the Christina River to mourn the loss of this great leader. Except for the wailing of the hired women, a heavy air of quietness and respect settled over the village and the surrounding camps.

[99] Jacob Alricks, the new director of New Amstel, as Fort Casimir was now called, arrived 27 April 1657 and died 30 December 1659. His nephew, Peter Alricks, replaced him in 1660.

Even the dogs stopped their yipping and yapping while the Lenape arrived at his wigwam and stood silently before the body.

The Lenape spared no expense to show proper respect for him. The Swedes' carpenter built him a smooth casket. They dressed him in new leggings and moccasins of deerskin embroidered with porcupine quills and small beads of various colors. He wore a new white shirt made of the finest duffel available. Draped diagonally across his chest lay the famous old red blanket with its black-striped bands, somewhat faded but still glorious. A few dashes of vermilion tastefully applied to the face, the black cravat around the neck with its gold clasp holding it close, the gold earrings, and the wide silver armbands contrasted colors in artistic beauty. Five wide belts of white wampum with a purple turtle carefully worked into each belt completed the stunning display. The belts lay lengthways across his body, angling from the right side to the left side of the coffin such that the turtle on the right side lay near his feet with each succeeding turtle on the next belt a bit higher, the whole thing giving the impression that the tortoise was moving upward toward his right hand. The tortoises moved toward a silver medallion lying in the open right palm of the great chieftain. Inscribed in unmistakeable clarity on the silver medallion stood the imprint of a tortoise with twelve divisions on its carapace.

On the day of the funeral, the family brought a few of the chief's personal belongings—his bow, three steel-tipped arrows, his tomahawk, his knife, a set of new clothes—and laid them in the coffin beside him; then they closed the lid. After they had shoved a small bag of vermilion paint through the hole in the end of the casket,[100] the funeral procession began.

[100] The hole in the end of the casket supposedly allowed the spirit of the deceased to go in and out at pleasure until it found the place of its future residence.

A guide stepped forward to lead the procession. Next, six warriors carried the corpse, followed closely by Falling Leaf. The principal chiefs and counselors of the nation came next in line, followed by all the men, and lastly the women and children. The chief mourners advanced about fifteen yards to the right of the corpse as they kept the air bleeding with their shrill cries. Whenever the pallbearers stopped to rest, the entire procession halted.

When the corpse arrived at the grave, the bearers rested it on the ground, and once more the attendants removed the lid from the coffin. The entire crowd seated themselves on the ground in a huge semicircle to one side of the casket. Inside the semicircle sat Falling Leaf and a few other close friends. On the opposite side of the grave from the crowd sat the mourners, their wailing stilled with only an occasional sigh or sob from them. Other than the muffled notes of grief from the mourners, the huge crowd sat in dead silence till the shadows began to lengthen again.

At last six men stepped forward to put the lid on the coffin and lower the body into the grave. Suddenly three of the chief mourners rushed forward to the dead chief and caressed his hands and legs while they cried, "Arise, arise! Come with us! Don't leave us! Don't abandon us! Arise, arise! Do not forsake us!" The three women finally retired from the body in a frenzied state of despair. They continued uttering loud cries while they plucked at their clothes, pulled their hair, and tore up shrubs and grass. Even after they had resumed their seats on the grass, their distraught cries continued while the six men closed the lid on the coffin and lowered the body into the grave.

After placing the body in the grave, the men next laid two debarked poles the thickness of a man's hand lengthways across the grave spaced a span apart. Falling Leaf walked across the grave on these poles and continued his very slow pace toward the east.

When Falling Leaf was no longer in sight from the grave, two men stepped forward carrying a pole on which was carved a progression of signs telling the story of the fallen chief's life. Meas (MEE us), a Lenape man of note, carefully placed the end of the pole on the head end of the coffin and made sure that the beginning and the ending of the inscription faced to the east.

The women covered the grave with dirt, tamped the post in place while Meas steadied it, and finally spread leaves and pieces of bark over the surface until no fresh ground was visible. After the women finished their task of closing the grave, men with prefitted timbers built a breast-high fence around the spot to keep wild beasts from disturbing it.

The ceremonies being ended, a complete cooked meal was served, and last of all, everyone present from the least to the greatest received a gift, with those who had done the most work receiving the largest gifts. The mourners received the largest gifts of all—a blanket, a ruffled shirt, a stroud, and leggings.

At dusk a kettle of victuals was carried to the grave and placed upon it. The same was done every evening for the space of three weeks until the spirit of the sachem supposedly had found his place of residence. For the entire three-week period after the burial, the wails of the mourners rent the evening stillness, the cries gradually diminishing in intensity until they were heard no more.

Glikkikan, the Lenape buried Mattahorn with the greatest honors possible. We revere and honor the memory of such a great sachem. We hold the burial places of our dead sacred and treat them with the utmost respect. No Lenape, no Indian, indeed, not even a Mengwe would ever have touched the grave of Mattahorn.

But shortly after the twenty-day care period with its daily visits was over, Mattahorn's grave was robbed and the silver tortoise stolen.

Narrated by Glikkikan

Owechela told me Mattahorn had to be one of the greatest leaders the Lenape ever had.

Mattahorn foresaw the inevitable consequences of the Schwannek onslaught with its advanced weapons and moral sickness.

He tried to balance the greed of the Dutch against the covetousness of the Swedes and the English.

Some Schwanneks went through the pretense of purchasing land from the Lenape and then claiming that their paper deeds gave them the right to drive the Lenape from their lands.

Other settlers made no pretense of purchase at all, but simply took the land and backed their advances into the Lenape homeland by force of arms.

Mattahorn always championed Lenape rights to their homeland. He insisted that all land deeds signed by the Lenape were only pacts allowing the Schwanneks to live in peace as guests of the Lenape.

At the same time Mattahorn struggled with the onslaught of the Schwanneks, he also tried to alert his own people to the danger they faced. He presided at the grand council fire at Shackamoxon and asked the Lenape to consider the complete destruction of the Swedes.[101]

Mattahorn saw Big Belly's weakness. Big Belly restrained his dealings with the Lenape only because of his lack of support with arms and trade goods from Sweden. Mattahorn understood. He matched Big Belly's bluster eyeball to eyeball.

To frighten the Lenape, Big Belly repeatedly told Mattahorn that he expected ships with a great many colonists and many supplies. Mattahorn was not fooled. When only a ship or two arrived with a few settlers, Mattahorn knew that the Swedes still lay within his power.

Mattahorn forged an alliance with the Susquehannocks. Using his friendship with Lasse Cock and Lasse Cock's keen tongue, he persuaded the Swedes to train and help arm the Susquehannocks.

Mattahorn understood that all the Mengwe talk about making women peacemakers out of the Lenape was only hot air backed by Dutch guns. The Mengwe didn't want peace. They wanted furs and power. And the Susquehannocks stood in their way.

Mattahorn forged an alliance between the Susquehannocks, the Swedes, and the Lenape against the Dutch and the Mengwe. That alliance staved off mastery by the Dutch and the Mengwe.

The future is seldom clear in the present. Mattahorn gazed into the future. What he saw and foretold has come to pass.

He was a great man: a sage, a seer, a sachem, and a savior to the Lenape.

Lenape orators have told of his vision and have sung of his

---

[101] This statement refers back to the time when Big Belly, Governor Printz, gravely threatened the destruction of all the Indians. Due to lack of funds and backing from Sweden, he was unable to carry out his threat.

deeds at many a festival and many a council fire. The events
that followed after Mattahorn bear witness that his vision, his
counsels, his hopes, and his fears rang true.

   He carried well the Spirit of Tamenend in the Land of the
Dawn.

Ode to Mattahorn

Owechela sang to me an ode to Mattahorn:
From a mother of the Turtle Clan was he born
To rise and tower o'er Lenape land.
His voice rang out through field and forest
And wafted o'er shining streams and bubbling brooks.
The hope and courage of Tamenend.
            Mattahorn carried the Spirit of Tamenend.

He loved his homeland to him given
By the Spirit in the heaven.
He kept the charge to hold it close
And guard its onward course.
            Mattahorn held his homeland close.

He did not let the Mengwe flatter chatter
      of skirt and hoe and kettle,
Lead him to doubt the Mengwe mettle of dark thoughts
      that settle on fur and murder, rum and drum,
Until Lenape be bereft of bean and maize and meat
      with nothing left to eat.
He fell upon their devious plan

and united three Lenape clan
To grab the Mengwe snake
  and tear its poison fang from out its head.
      Mattahorn ripped the fang from out the Mengwe head.

When Big Belly threatened Mattahorn with war,
He threw his tomahawk upon the floor
  and warned the giant he must bend and bow
Or he would take the hatchet now
  and stick it in his head.
Thus he drove the raging bear back within his lair.
      Mattahorn drove the bear back into his lair.

He saw that Dutch and English, Swede and Finn,
  could not live in peace among their kin.
Thus he knew what they would do to men
  with reddish skin.
So he did perform a feat and did with
  Swede and Susquehannock treat
To unseat the Dutch and English fleet.
He did defeat the Strutting Turkey and
  brought him down.
      Mattahorn brought the Turkey down.

He let the Turkey hold sway if he would obey
  and not drive the Swedes away.
But when Mercurius arrived, the Turkey forgot
  and said he would not
  let the ship pass the mark
  or the settlers disembark.
When the De Waag came around, Mattahorn ran it aground
  and bent forty cannon barrels down.

Then at last, as it flew its flag of yellow and blue,
  he sailed the Mercurius past.
    Mattahorn bent barrels down and rode the
      Mercurius past.

He carried well up to the end
The courageous Spirit of Tamenend.
Now there are no treaties to amend or borders to defend,
Now his spirit roams at will to tend the happy land of
  Tamenend.
    Mattahorn's dove soars above the land of Tamenend.

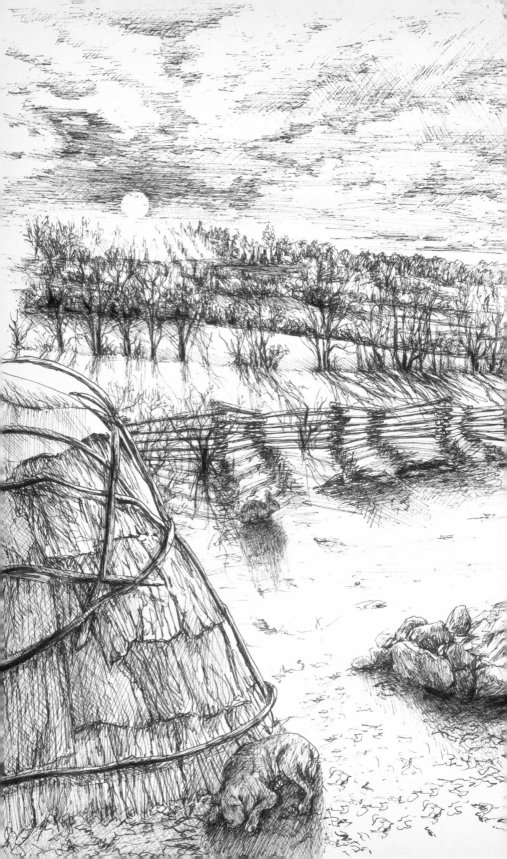

"My homeland"

–Glikkikan in Peace Valley

CQ108

Cast of Main Characters

Bad Dog Hossitt—Gillis Hossitt, head of the first (1632) Dutch colony at Swanendael (Lewes, Delaware).

Bent Stick Grasmeer—Wilhelmus Grasmeer, a minister in the Dutch Reformed Church who conducted services for Governor Stuyvesant from 1651 to 1652.

Big Belly Printz—Johan Printz, a blustery former general who ruled the Swedish colony on the Delaware from 1642 to 1653.

Champ Gun Champlain—Samuel De Champlain, a French trader who founded Quebec City in 1608 and aided the Algonquian tribes in a raid on the Mengwe.

Commander Jacquet—Jean Paul Jacquet, Dutch commander at Fort Casimir (1656) who colluded with Falling Leaf.

Elder Eesanques—A Lenape elder from the Siconece present at the coming of the white man at Manhattan and Swanendael.

Ever-Be-Joyful—A grieving Lenape mother who helped bring about peace between the Lenape and the Cherokees.

Falling Leaf Cock—Lasse Cock, a Swedish lad whose life included trader, translator, Indian agent, and advocate.

Glikkikan—A young Lenape boy being trained as an orator by his grandfather, Patriarch Owechela.

Madman Kieft—William Kieft (1597-1647), Dutch governor at New Amsterdam responsible for genocide against the Indians.

Sachem Mattahorn—A head Lenape chief who sought to preserve his people by allying the Lenape, Swedes, and

Susquehannocks against the Dutch and Mengwe.

Morning Light Rising—Johan Rising (1617-1672), an enlightened Swedish governor who restored friendly relations with the Indians.

Patriarch Owechela—An aged Lenape chief tells the story of his people to his grandson, Glikkikan.

Captain Papegoja—Swedish commander of Fort Christina and son-in-law of Governor Johan Printz.

Pastor Green Leaf Campanius—John Companius Holm (1601-1683), Swedish pastor who learned Lenape and mediated between Lenape and Swedes from 1643 to 1648.

Poconguigula—A young Lenape brave who bound an Erie strong man and helped bring peace between the two nations.

Strong Friend—The chief who led the first contingent across the Mississippi and was humiliated by the Alligéwi.

Strutting Turkey Stuyvesant—Peter Stuyvesant, an aggressive Dutch governor of New Amsterdam from 1647 to 1664. He conquered the Swedes on the Delaware.

Oracle Tamenend—The Lenni Lenape leader who received the gift of the Land of the Dawn from the Great Spirit.

Peace Tamanend—An early Lenape chief who championed peace instead of fighting.

Shaman Teotacken—A highly regarded Lenape chief and medicine man thought to have great power over evil spirits.

Turn Coat Minuit—Peter Minuit directed the Dutch colony of New Netherland between 1626 and 1631. He switched to the Swedish and founded New Sweden in 1638. In the same year he was lost at sea.

Place Names

Christina–Wilmington, Delaware
Drunk Island–Manhattan Island, New York City
Fort Altena–Wilmington, Delaware
Fort Casimir–New Castle, Delaware
Fort Nassau–Gloucester City, New Jersey
Hoerenkill–Whore's Creek. Today: Lewes, Delaware
Lenape Bay–Delaware Bay
Lenape River–Delaware River
Manahachtánienk–Manhattan Island, New York City
Matennecunk Isle–Delaware River, Burlington, New Jersey
Minquas Kill–Christina River, Wilmington, Delaware
New Amstel–New Castle, Delaware
New Amsterdam–New York City
North River–Hudson River, New York State
Passayunk–Schuylkill River, Philadelphia, Pennsylvania
Shackamoxon–Kensington, Philadelphia, Pennsylvania
Siconece Creek–Lewes Creek, Lewes, Delaware
South River–Delaware River: edge of Delaware & Pennsylvania
Suppeckongh–Christina Kill, Wilmington, Delaware
Swanendael–Valley of Swans. Today: Lewes, Delaware
The Place Where We All Got Drunk–Manhattan, NYC
Tinicum Island–Due east of Chester, Pennsylvania

Languages and Nations

We want to think for a moment about the confusing array of nations (tribes) and languages mentioned in *Lenape Homeland*. In such a study, one cannot escape how language has so much to do with culture, religion, and friendship.

If we cannot talk freely with others, we tend to mistrust them rather than understand them. I have experienced this fear and doubt in foreign countries. Can I trust them? Can they trust me?

The same is true among nations. If nations have similar languages, they usually get along together. Nations that have different languages often try to overpower others speaking an unfamiliar tongue.

In *Lenape Homeland* we see how the European nations so often fought with each other and were classed by what language they spoke—French, English, Spanish, Dutch, Swedish. The same difficulty of getting along existed between the Mengwe and the Lenape, who spoke two different root languages.

The Lenape, Shawnee, and Mohicans mentioned in this book all belonged to the great Algonquin language family that extended from Labrador westward through Canada to the Rocky Mountains and southward to South Carolina. And of all the Algonquin family, the Lenape were the greatest. I quote from *Handbook of the Delaware Indian Language* by Scott

Hayes Wenning: "It is said that forty tribes looked up to the Lenape with respect, and that, in the great councils of the Algonquins, they took first place as 'grandfathers' of the race, while others were called by them 'children,' 'grandchildren,' and 'nephews.' ... And it seems true that the Algonquin tribes refrained from war with one another."

The Mengwe were not an Algonquin-speaking people. Five nations in this language family known today as Iroquian—Mohawk, Oneida, Onondaga, Cayuga, and the Seneca—formed a confederation in 1570 and were called Five Nations by the English, Maquas by the Dutch, and Iroquois by the French. Some other nations in this language group were the Tuscaroras, Cherokees, Eries, Wyandots, and Hurons.

Keep in mind, then, as you think about the coming of the Whites to the Lenape River Valley, that language was as important to the Indian nations as it was to the European nations who invaded their country.

Fact or Fiction?

Right from the beginning, whenever I started talking about the book I was researching and writing, one of the first questions that came up in one form or another was, "Is The Conquest Series fiction or nonfiction?"

Earl Olmstead, author of two books on David Zeisberger, asked, "Are you going to write fiction or nonfiction?"

My wife wanted to know: "Is it true? Did this really happen?"

Every prospective publisher asks whether this book is fiction or nonfiction.

The genre of The Conquest Series is historical novel. A historical novel means that a fictitious story is based on recorded facts.

The Conquest Series is history. Most of the characters once lived, and many of the events portrayed really happened. Where deemed advisable, I have footnoted actual dates and given explanations in order to maintain historical integrity.

But let us remember that historians often find different "facts" or err in the "facts" they record. I am no different.

Even with careful searching, some records have eluded my research. Therefore it is quite likely that some "facts" in The Conquest Series will turn out to be inaccurate. This cannot be helped. But my wish is that the reader of The Conquest Series might confidently assume the story does not violate any known facts.

But history is much more than a written record of recorded

"facts." In a sense, all of recorded history is only an imaginary written record of what the scribe *believed* to be true.

If you were to ask ten different observers what time the sun came up this morning, you would likely get ten different answers. Viewed from each observer's platform, the sun rose at different times. Historians view the "facts" the same way.

For instance, take the "fact" of the purchase of Manhattan from the Indians for a few trinkets. From a Dutch observer's viewpoint it might be toted as "the best real estate buy in all history." In the eyes of a Lenape observer the same "fact" was murderous robbery.

The colored lenses of every writer of history slants the "facts" the way he sees them. These are the colored lenses through which I slant The Conquest Series:

- My personal faith has been Christian and of the Mennonite persuasion from my youth up to my present seventy-three years of age.
- I believe the Bible presents an unchanging, absolute standard of right and wrong rather than a relative one that changes with the times.
- I have an intense interest in the land (ownership, stewardship, and productivity), in history (Anabaptist and American), and in freedom (individual, economic, religious, and political).

But The Conquest Series is more than a careful recording of biographical details and "facts" from the writer's viewpoint. It is a made-up story. It is fiction.

There is no historical record of any of the medallions. I

made them up and used them as a device to grip the reader and hold him in the story from one end to the other. But you should know that everything the medallions represented was true, and, I believe, presented accurately in the story.

I "know" only a few words of Lenape and never met any of the characters portrayed; I imagined every conversation, every song, and every poem because I wrote in English. None of it was a translation taken from documents written in Lenape.

Yet I believe this carefully crafted story presents a true history of how characters thought and felt about the recorded events.

If it were possible to resurrect some eminent historians of the period such as John Heckewelder, C. A. Weslager, Amandus Johnson, Daniel G. Brinton, and Francis Jennings, I believe they would agree with the conclusions offered in The Conquest Series, for it is from the threads of their writings that I have woven this story.

The Conquest Series, then, is history. It is slanted nonfiction; it is true.

The Conquest Series is also fiction, because I imagined what the characters said and felt and thought during their few days of life under the sun.

In The Conquest Series I strive to portray the face and heart of every character consistent with all records and human action known to me.

I hope you will find this recipe, blending total fiction and believed facts, gourmet reading.

My Passion

When I first read the story of Isaac Glikkikan, I already had enough training and experience as a writer to recognize the makings of a great story.

Three "why" questions about Isaac Glikkikan's life intrigued me: Why would a renowned, heathen war chief give his heart to the Lord Jesus Christ and become a Praying Indian? Why did Glikkikan lay down the knife and tomahawk and power and respect to be despised by the people of his own nation? Why did he remain true to his Lord even unto death by a cooper's mallet?

I set out to bring Isaac Glikkikan back to life so he could answer those questions for me. But, as John Donne wrote, "No man is an island entire of itself." I soon found out that if I were to bring Glikkikan back with a heart and a face and a spirit, I also had to raise up other characters who made Isaac Glikkikan the man he was.

As I resurrected the characters in this book from the graves of a bygone era, they took on lives of their own. No longer could I dangle them from strings as puppets and make them do and dance by the taps of my fingers on the keyboard.

No longer were these characters only tin soldiers, plastic saints, brass savages, and wooden frontiersmen—pallid characters of little interest or usefulness. They now wanted to do things their own way.

At such times I could lean forward as I wrote, anxious to

watch the unfolding seventeenth-century drama. I wanted
to know what Tamenend, Eesanques, Mattahorn, Meas, and
Glikkikan would do next, and how the story would unfold.

The next thing I noticed was that many characters
throughout the series became strangely familiar to me. They
reminded me of people I had met years ago but whose names I
couldn't quite remember.

Not only characters seemed familiar, but today's events
started to sound like echoes from 350 years ago.

The Clintonian raid on the Branch Davidians sounded like
Governor Kieft's murder of the Mohicans.

Hitler's "Final Solution" echoed the phrase begun by
Nathaniel Bacon: "The only good Indian is a dead Indian."

My heart went out to Cool Water and Friend Dreamer.
I struggled with ungodly anger at Little Heron and Great
Heron. My mind strained with Meas and Mattahorn as they
sought to see beyond the deadly moment. I wished them to
conquer evil with good.

The story gripped my life and became a penetrating passion.

I hope that the tale of The Conquest Series will also grip
your feelings and cause you to empathize with Eesanques,
Ever-Be-Joyful, Mattahorn, Meas, Cool Water, and Glikkikan
in their worldly struggle between good and evil.

I pray that The Conquest Series will help you avoid some of
the horrible mistakes made by frail men of the past, as well as
lift up giants of good for you to follow.

And most of all, I hope that you, too, will find out why
Isaac Glikkikan traded hate and a hatchet for a cross and a
crown.

Confessions of the Author

I confess that I am not a professional writer. This is only my second book. The first one, *You Can Write*, remained on my bestseller list for fifteen years before selling out the first printing of five hundred copies.

I do not know everything about anything, and that includes Delaware Indian history. If you find an inaccuracy, mistake, or some other writer malfunction, charge it to my account.

I confess that I knew nothing about the life story of Glikkikan until I read about him in Peter Hoover's book, *The Secret of the Strength*. Brother Peter gets the credit for encouraging me to write this book and personally escorting me to Bethlehem, Pennsylvania, to get me started.

I also must confess that researching and writing this story took much longer than the two years I had forecasted when I first began the project. Without Doris (my serious-minded wife who doesn't read fiction) I'd never have made it. Her highest compliment when she read along was, "Did that really happen or are you just making it up?"

I confess that sometimes I did make things up. But often I found the truth so strange that I had to insert footnotes just to convince Doris she really was reading history.

I confess that I am not a professional researcher. I have spent little time sifting through the sacred precincts of archives in search of unpublished manuscripts. And I feared to bother the professionals with my elementary questions. Yet some professionals did respond kindly to my amateur ways—Michael Depaolo at the Lewes Historical Society, Lewes, Delaware; Mike Dixon at the Elkton Historical Society, Elkton, Maryland; Ed Chichirichi at the Delaware History Center, Wilmington, Delaware; Brian Cannon and Cindy Snyder at the New Castle Courthouse Museum, New Castle, Delaware; Lois Burkholder at the Menno Simons Historical Library, Harrisonburg, Virginia; and Dr. Peter Craig, F.A.S.G., Washington, D.C. I owe them my thanks.

I must confess that I knew little about Lenape history or culture when I began this study. However, the wonders of the age have literally brought the Lenape and Colonial worlds to my studio. More than 140 books and manuscripts related to this subject line my shelves, almost all of them selected from catalogs and online offerings. Hundreds and perhaps thousands of people I never met have helped me—Internet technicians, authors, publishers, printers, and computer whizzes. In Mark Twain's cryptic words, "This work is tainted with the work of others. 'Tain't mine alone."

Furthermore, I confess that in ideal weather I can barely type forty words per minute. And when I'm writing a story, I can barely get forty words per hour. Without an iMac ... I don't even like to think about it.

And I confess that I've thoroughly enjoyed every aspect of writing this story.

Well now I've " 'fessed up." Like the old saying goes, "Confession is good for the soul." 'Tis true.

Bibliography – Vol. I

Primary Sources

Adams, Richard C., ed. *Legends of the Delaware Indians and Picture Writing.* Original–Washington D.C., 1905: N.p. Published–Syracuse, NY: Syracuse University Press, 1997.

Brinton, Daniel G. *The Lenape and Their Legends.* Philadelphia, PA, 1885. Reprinted: Lewisburg, PA: Wennawoods Publishing, 1999.

Heckewelder, John. *History, Manners, and Customs of the Indian Nations.* Philadelphia, PA: The Historical Society of Pennsylvania, 1876.

Johnson, Amandus. *The Swedes on the Delaware 1638-1664.* Philadelphia, PA: International Printing Company, 1927.

Pritchard, Evan T. *No Word for Time, the Way of the Algonquin People.* San Francisco, CA/Tulsa, OK: Council Oak Books, 1997.

Sipe, C. Hale. *The Indian Chiefs of Pennsylvania.* Butler, PA, 1927. Reprinted: Lewisburg, PA: Wennawoods Publishing, 1994.

Weslager, C.A. *The Delaware Indians-A History.* New Brunswick, NJ: Rutgers University Press, 1972.

Weslager, C.A. & Dunlap, A.R. *Dutch Explorers, Traders and Settlers in the Delaware Valley 1609-1664.* Philadelphia, PA: University of Pennsylvania Press, 1961.

Weslager, C.A. *The English on the Delaware 1610-1682.* New Brunswick, NJ: Rutgers University Press, 1967.

Weslager, C.A. *The Siconese Indians of Lewes, Delaware.* Lewes, DE: Lewes Historical Society, 1991.

Weslager, C.A. *The Swedes and Dutch at New Castle.* Bart, New York: The Middle Atlantic Press, 1987.

General Sources

Acrelius, Israel. Translation and notes by Reynolds, William M. *A History of New Sweden; or The Settlements on the River Delaware.* Philadelphia, PA: The Historical Society of Pennsylvania, 1874.

Albensi, Bill. *Lenape and the Colony of New Sweden.* Wilmington, DE: Nopoly Press, Inc., 1987.

Barsotti, John J. *Scoouwa.* Columbus, OH: Ohio Historical Society, 1978. Original: Bradford, John. *An Account of the Remarkable Occurrences in the Life and Travels of Col. James Smith.* Lexington, MA, 1799.

Cohen, William J. *Swanendael in New Netherland.* Wilmington, DE: Cedar Tree Books, Ltd., 2004.

Donehoo, Dr. George P. *A History of the Indian Villages and Place Names in Pennsylvania.* Harrisburg, PA, 1928. Reprinted: Lewisburg, PA: Wennawoods Publishing, 1998.

Footner, Hulbert. *Rivers of the Eastern Shore.* Cambridge, MD: Tidewater Publishers, 1944.

Frank, Albert H. *Transactions of the Moravian Historical Society.*
Vol. 26: "Spiritual Life in Schoenbrunn Village," Nazareth,
PA, 1990.

Grumet, Robert S. *The Lenapes.* New York, NY; Philadelphia,
PA: Chelsea House Publishers, 1989.

Harrington, M.R. *The Indians of New Jersey, Dickon Among the
Lenapes.* New Brunswick, NJ: Rutgers University Press,
1963. Original: Holt, Rinehart and Winston, Inc., 1938.

Heckewelder, John. *Narrative of the Mission of the United
Brethren Among ... Indians, 1740-1808.* Philadelphia, PA:
McCarty and Davis, 1820. Reprint: Arno Press, 1971.

Heckewelder, John. *The First American Frontier.* Arno Press
and The New York Times, 1971.

Holm, Thomas Campanius, translated by Du Ponceau, Peter
S. *Description of the Province of New Sweden.* Philadelphia, PA:
McCarty & Davis, 1834.

Jacobs, Wilbur R. *Diplomacy and Indian Gifts, Anglo-French
Rivalry Along the Ohio and Northwest Frontiers, 1748-1763.*
Original: Stanford, CA, 1950. Reprint: Lewisburg, PA:
Wennawoods Publishing, 2001.

Jennings, Francis. *The Ambiguous Iroquois Empire.* New York,
NY: W. W. Norton & Company, 1984.

Jennings, Francis. *The Founders of America.* New York, NY:
W. W. Norton & Company, 1993.

Jennings, Francis. *The Invasion of America.* New York, NY: W.
W. Norton & Company, 1975.

Kraft, Herbert C. *The Lenape or Delaware Indians.* South
Orange, NJ: Seton Hall University Museum, 1996.

Mancall, Peter C. *Deadly Medicine.* Ithaca, NY: Cornell

University Press, 1995.

Mcintosh, John. *The Origin of the North American Indians.* New York, NY: Nafis & Cornish, 1844.

McLuhan, T. C. *Touch the Earth.* London, Great Britain: Garnstone Press, Ltd., 1972.

McNeal, Patricia. *Painters of the First Frontier,* compiled from *Westsylvania Stories.* Gettysburg, PA: Lord Nelson's Art Gallery, 2002.

Merrell, James H. *Into the American Woods.* New York & London: W. W. Norton & Company, 1999.

Myers, Albert Cook, ed. *William Penn's Own Account of the Lenni Lenape or Delaware Indians.* Wilmington, DE: The Middle Atlantic Press, 1970.

Olmstead, Earl P. *David Zeisberger–A Life among the Indians.* Kent, Ohio: The Kent State University Press, 1997.

O'Neil, James F., comp. and ed. *Their Bearing Is Noble and Proud.* Dayton, OH: J.T.G.S. Publishing, 1995.

Paterek, Josephine. *Encyclopedia of American Indian Costume.* New York, NY: W. W. Norton & Company, 1994.

Shoemaker, Henry W., comp. *A Pennsylvania Bison Hunt.* Middleburg, PA, 1915. Reprinted: Lewisburg, PA: Wennawoods Publishing, 1998.

Smith, Craig Stephen. *Whiteman's Gospel.* Winnipeg, Manitoba: Indian Life Books, 1997.

Tantaquidgeon, Gladys. *Folk Medicine of the Delaware and Related Algonkian Indians.* Harrisburg, PA: Commonwealth of Pennsylvania, 1972.

Tehanetorens. *Wampum Belts,* Onchiota, NY: Six Nations Indian Museum, 1972.

Turdo, Mark A. *Common People, Uncommon Community Lenape Life in Moravian Missions.* Nazareth, PA: Moravian Historical Society, 1998.

Walker, Bryce, chief ed. *Through Indian Eyes.* Pleasantville, NY: The Reader's Digest Association, 1995.

Wallace, Paul A. W. *Indian Paths of Pennsylvania.* Harrisburg, PA: The Pennsylvania Historical Commission, 1965.

Wallace, Paul A. W. *Indians in Pennsylvania.* Commonwealth of Pennsylvania, 1961. Reprint: Harrisburg, PA, 1999.

Wallace, Paul A. W., ed. *Thirty Thousand Miles with John Heckewelder.* Published 1958. Reprinted: Lewisburg, PA: Wennawoods Publishing, 1998.

Wenning, Scott Hayes. *Handbook of the Delaware Indian Language.* Lewisburg, PA: Wennawoods Publishing, 2000.

Wilson, Dorothy Clarke. *Bright Eyes.* New York, NY: McGraw-Hill Book Company, 1974.

Witthoft, John. *The American Indian as Hunter.* Harrisburg, PA: Commonwealth of Pennsylvania Historical and Museum Commission, 1999.

Zeisberger, David. Archer Butler Hulbert and William Nathaniel Schwarze, ed. *David Zeisberger's History of the Northern American Indians.* Marietta, OH: Ohio State Archaeological and Historical Society, 1910. Reprint: Lewisburg, PA: Wennawoods Publishing, 1999.

Zeisberger, David. *Journals & Diaries of David Zeisberger.* Gathered by Earl Olmstead, Kent State, OH, 1988.

About the Author

by Fonda Joy Wadel

L ove for learning sparked early in my dad's life.
Raised on Pennsylvania and Virginia farms by a professor father and a home-loving mother, his world formed in a place where work and study intermingled. Reading and history lessons captured his young mind in class while farm chores educated his hands at home.

After graduating from high school in 1960, Dad chose agricultural work for three years. But the yearning for book learning propelled him on to college. For another year he sharpened English composition skills and reveled in Bible and history lessons.

Dad enlarged his education with diverse experiences. For fourteen years he dairy farmed on Georgia plains. He taught high school students amid Pennsylvania hills. He wrote at a publishing house in the New Mexico desert.

From his West Virginia mountain home he edited educational newsletters and penned articles for farm magazines. Hobbies varied from chess games and singing to beekeeping, landscaping, and composting.

His agricultural, economic, and historical interests spurred travel to Central and South America, Europe, Africa, Australia, and New Zealand.

Dad prizes truth. He refuses to accept pat answers flipped to ethical questions. His beliefs demand Bible research, historical evaluation, and worldview consideration. He enjoys stirring minds through church periodicals, Sunday school classes, and Bible history lessons.

Dad's manifesto flies above the hearts of all seven of his children: *Drink knowledge. Hail adventure. Stand on truth.*

Christian Aid Ministries

Christian Aid Ministries was founded in 1981 as a non-profit, tax-exempt 501(c)(3) organization. Its primary purpose is to provide a trustworthy and efficient channel for Amish, Mennonite, and other conservative Anabaptist groups and individuals to minister to physical and spiritual needs around the world. This is in response to the command to ". . . do good unto all men, especially unto them who are of the household of faith" (Galatians 6:10).

Each year, CAM supporters provide approximately 15 million pounds of food, clothing, medicines, seeds, Bibles, Bible story books, and other Christian literature for needy people. Most of the aid goes to orphans and Christian families. Supporters' funds also help to clean up and rebuild for natural disaster victims, put up Gospel billboards in the U.S., support several church-planting efforts, operate two medical clinics, and provide resources for needy families to make their own living. CAM's main purposes for providing aid are to help and encourage God's people and bring the Gospel to a lost and dying world.

CAM has staff, warehouses, and distribution networks in Romania, Moldova, Ukraine, Haiti, Nicaragua, Liberia, and Israel. Aside from management, supervisory personnel, and bookkeeping operations, volunteers do most of the work at CAM locations. Each year, volunteers at our warehouses, field bases, Disaster Response Services projects, and other locations donate over 200,000 hours of work.

CAM's ultimate purpose is to glorify God and help enlarge His kingdom. ". . . whatsoever ye do, do all to the glory of God" (1 Corinthians 10:31).

The Way to God and Peace

We live in a world contaminated by sin. Sin is anything that goes against God's holy standards. When
we do not follow the guidelines that God our
Creator gave us, we are guilty of sin. Sin separates us from
God, the source of life.

Since the time when the first man and woman, Adam and
Eve, sinned in the Garden of Eden, sin has been universal.
The Bible says that we all have "sinned and come short of
the glory of God" (Romans 3:23). It also says that the natural
consequence for that sin is eternal death, or punishment in
an eternal hell: "Then when lust hath conceived, it bringeth
forth sin: and sin, when it is finished, bringeth forth death"
(James 1:15).

But we do not have to suffer eternal death in hell. God pro-
vided forgiveness for our sins through the death of His only
Son, Jesus Christ. Because Jesus was perfect and without sin,
He could die in our place. "For God so loved the world that
he gave his only begotten Son, that whosoever believeth in
him should not perish, but have everlasting life" (John 3:16).

A sacrifice is something given to benefit someone else. It
costs the giver greatly. Jesus was God's sacrifice. Jesus' death
takes away the penalty of sin for everyone who accepts this sacrifice and truly repents of their sins. To repent of sins means
to be truly sorry for and turn away from the things we have
done that have violated God's standards (Acts 2:38; 3:19).

Jesus died, but He did not remain dead. After three days,
God's Spirit miraculously raised Him to life again. God's Spirit
does something similar in us. When we receive Jesus as our

sacrifice and repent of our sins, our hearts are changed. We become spiritually alive! We develop new desires and attitudes (2 Corinthians 5:17). We begin to make choices that please God (1 John 3:9). If we do fail and commit sins, we can ask God for forgiveness. "If we confess our sins, he is faithful and just to forgive us our sins, and to cleanse us from all unrighteousness" (1 John 1:9).

Once our hearts have been changed, we want to continue growing spiritually. We will be happy to let Jesus be the Master of our lives and will want to become more like Him. To do this, we must meditate on God's Word and commune with God in prayer. We will testify to others of this change by being baptized and sharing the good news of God's victory over sin and death. Fellowship with a faithful group of believers will strengthen our walk with God (1 John 1:7).